# In the Shadow of a Giant - a Novelette

*Sci-Fi tale of noble houses' epic starship battles, political intrigue, sabotage, betrayal, revenge, and, ultimately, survival in a decaying galactic empire*

## Joseph Graff

**Perfect Publishing**

Copyright © 2024 Joseph Graff

All rights reserved

The characters and events portrayed in this book are fictitious. Any similarity to real persons, living or dead, is coincidental and not intended by the author.

No part of this book may be reproduced, or stored in a retrieval system, or transmitted in any form or by any means, electronic, mechanical, photocopying, recording, or otherwise, without express written permission of the publisher.

ISBN-13: 9798343981933

Cover design by: Art Painter
Library of Congress Control Number: 2018675309
Printed in the United States of America

# CONTENTS

| | |
|---|---|
| Title Page | |
| Copyright | |
| In the Shadow of a Giant | 1 |
| Make a Difference with Your Review | 21 |
| Keeping the Adventure Alive | 49 |
| About The Author | 51 |
| Praise For Author | 55 |
| Books By This Author | 59 |
| BONUS Excerpt from: SSSSnake Jokessss, Riddlessss & Rattlessss - by and for kids | 63 |
| What if the last hope for humanity lay in the hands of machines? | 67 |
| BONUS Excerpt from: The Last Stand of the Golems | 69 |
| BONUS Excerpt from: The Ten Human Homeworlds | 75 |
| BONUS Excerpt from: Joesephianism Inc. (Un)Official Wiki | 81 |
| BONUS Excerpt from: God-engines | 93 |
| BONUS Excerpt from: Joffe nezum Official Wiki (No). | 99 |
| Perfect Publishing - Sci-fi, Horror, Trivia, Comedy, Satire, Jokes, Music, Health/Fitness/Longevity | 107 |

# IN THE SHADOW OF A GIANT

*A Novelette by Joseph Graff*

The convoy sailed in the shadow of a giant. Both remnants of an empire long since past. One, a set of tiny thruster flames against a colossal gray silhouette, was a flotilla of merchant starships with a light military escort. Piracy was frequent in these territories, especially so since the fall of the Old Empire, but the star lanes were plied all the same. Food, water, raw materials, all goods needed to be transported, and the risk of transporting them did not change this fact. It only increased the benefit for those rare commanders who were willing to risk their ships transporting them.

The other, a massive triangular pyramid nearly five hundred kilometers from end to end, was a space city. One of the last bastions of civilization after the inhabited worlds were mostly turned desolate. Every day, its billions of inhabitants ate and defecated and consumed valuable resources of which there was only a finite supply. When the Old Empire ceased to exist, nearly a century prior, the city's supply chain was lost along with it. The nearby asteroid fields soon ran dry of resources. The food stores were replaced with growth vats, each one consuming as much power and water as five people. The beating heart of the city began to slow down.

This was why the merchant fleets existed. Thousands of ships, with millions of souls aboard, braving treacherous space for weeks at a time in order to feed and clothe the unwashed masses. The space city's administration had promised to use the influx of resources to build warships to fend off the fearsome fleets of marauders that plagued the local star cluster. But the pressures of fending off starvation were too much to bear. The fleet yards had not produced a ship in nearly thirty years.

Ninety percent of the city's merchant and military ships were relics from the Old Empire, passed down from generation to generation in a revival of the feudal societies of Earth. Commodores became dukes. Admirals became kings. Crews became peasants, sold and traded as easily as the ships they called home. For some, serving under cruel masters, the conditions were worse than being enslaved by the pirates. Mutinies usually occurred soon after.

This merchant fleet, which had just now slipped its moorings to seek riches among the stars, had no such concerns. Its crews were well-fed and cared for, and its ruling commodore was a kind and just man. That was a far nobler virtue than one might think, because this world was cruel to men who were kind. Commodore Gideon Adira knew this fact well.

"Attention, Space City Albion, this is the convoy Fulcrum. Please confirm our transit permit," his communications officer rattled off. The bridge of the convoy's flagship, an ancient destroyer christened Adamant Truth by its first and most famous captain, was a large and spacious room positioned near the stern of the ship. Its walls and roof were nearly entirely made of layered ironglass, a transparent metal that could only be produced in labs, and they gave a wonderful view over the top hull of the ship.

"Confirm transit permit," the communications officer repeated.

"Convoy Fulcrum, hold for further instructions," came the response. "Confirming with Transit Control now."

Space City Albion was a nation in constant decline. Corruption and nepotism had crippled its top ranks, the station's governor enriching himself like a greedy king of old, and the cancers it brought had crippled every aspect of Albion's functionality. The confirmation process was no different.

"Decelerate to a full stop," ordered the commodore. "I want a full systems check performed as well. We have time to wait."

In Albion, one's welfare and the welfare of their family depended largely on social status. Men from a venerable line, like that of the station governor or the more prominent admirals, could open doors simply by speaking their family name. Men of less important heritage, such as the commodore of Fulcrum convoy, were not nearly as lucky. And the line of Adira was poor indeed.

"Yes, Commodore Gideon," snapped his liaison. She was one of the rare liaisons who did not graduate from the Alabaster School, the training academy where young men and women learned how best to serve their noble employers. A good liaison had to serve as an aide, a spymaster, a bodyguard, and as many or as few other things as their master required. They were rare to find and expensive to hire, precisely why the Adira family had not hired a qualified liaison. Even the most affordable liaison's salary would cost half their yearly income, so Elena Zalle was the best they could hope to have. She interfaced with a neural implant, running a thousand calculations a second to execute Commodore Gideon's orders.

"Mass driver six reports an error," she informed her commander. "And A.F.S. Bulkhead reports minor engine trouble. Their maintenance teams are already responding."

The ore hauler Bulkhead had been refitted to house refineries on board, and her engines were among the systems that had to make cuts. It was only through the brilliance of the Adira family's engineers that the Bulkhead could move at all.

"Bring up a diagram of driver six," Commodore Gideon ordered. It was done. A translucent hologram of the blocky gun appeared in the air in front of him. "There," he said, pointing at a faulty magnetic coil in the weapon's barrel. "I thought we fixed that."

Railguns were primitive weapons, mass drivers even more so. Only the poorest and most ignominious family fleets fielded such batteries, and those who could not afford to maintain them were practically paupers.

"We did, sir," Liaison Zalle reported. Her uniform was white, notably lacking the three golden bars of the Alabaster School graduates, and her blonde hair was tied neatly behind her. "The fix didn't hold."

Commodore Gideon, in contrast to his liaison, had a dark blue uniform and straight black hair. A bird of prey with wings outstretched, the Adira family crest, was emblazoned upon his chest and inlaid in gray on each of his gold pauldrons. The animal itself, a formidable predator from a long-dead world, was now almost extinct. Gideon Adira owned the last remaining specimen.

The characteristic Adira family officer's cap sat firmly on Gideon' head, and a bejeweled scepter was clasped in his left hand.

"Very well, then," he sighed, closing the diagram of mass driver six. "Order the maintenance teams to tread vacuum and fix it up."

The Adira family prided itself on two things; integrity and discipline. They drilled their personnel to a level that was unmatched among the minor noble families. Any ship with a Adira crew, even if it had already changed hands many times, was considered among the most valuable in its class. The Adira family had been forced to sell many of these ships in hard times, only to purchase other models with inferior crews when their efforts proved profitable again.

Commodore Gideon, like his father, Commodore Alexander, had spent long and tireless hours training these crews up to Adira standards. It was one of the few tasks he refused to delegate to Liaison Zalle.

"Confirm," said the liaison. "Maintenance unit en route."

Within moments, a unit of gray-suited figures were emerging from an airlock near the dorsal gun battery. Armed with mechanic's tools and spare parts, they set to work on one of the Adamant's colossal guns. The repair was simple, a common fix for crews assigned to electromagnetic weapons, but the Adira crew impressed their master with how fast they got it done.

"Liaison Zalle?" he asked. She turned to face him. "See to it that those men receive a bonus for their work."

The Adira family always rewarded good service. That was part of the reason why they saw so much of it.

Finally, the glacial bureaucracy of Space City Albion finished its assigned task.

"Fulcrum convoy, this is Transit Control," a dull voice droned through the communications system. "Your permit is confirmed. Safe travels."

More often than not, they were anything but.

"Acknowledged, Transit Control," the communications officer responded. "Commodore?"

"Full ahead. Continue on course." The Adira convoy's engines burned back to life. Thruster plumes longer than the ships they came from lit up the sky like a meteor shower. Among the noble families of Space City Albion, the Adiras were poor, weak, and pathetic. But to the humble commoner, who had never played the game of politics and never seen munitions slam into the hulls of ships, the convoy looked as mighty as a fleet of the Old Empire itself.

"We're passing beyond the Rubicon Perimeter, sir," the navigation officer reported. "Any orders?"

The Rubicon Perimeter was an imaginary sphere around Space City Albion beyond which its defensive batteries could not reach. Within the perimeter, the Adira fleet enjoyed protection from rank after rank of mammoth guns and missile batteries. Beyond it, however, was lawless space. The authority of Albion stretched only as far as its power to enforce it, and that power stopped at the Rubicon Perimeter.

"Stay on course. Continue to the coordinates we've been sent." The Adira family, though poor and ignominious, was not without allies. Their honest and loyal nature, rare among the noble families of Albion, had won them the trust and respect of many powerful men and women. One such individual, a man without ships but not lacking in spies, had discovered the coordinates of an asteroid cluster rich in resources. The Adiras' enemies knew this location as well, and Gideon Adira had spent valuable resources making sure his fleet would reach it first.
Two hundred kilometers behind him and falling away fast, the mining ships of Ivan Morozov and his terrible kin lingered uselessly in dry dock. Adira family saboteurs had placed explosives in their engines. The Morozov armada would not fly again for some weeks, and that was plenty of time for Gideon Adira and his men to strip their prize dry of valuable ore.

"Commodore Gideon!" the communications officer announced in shock. "We're being hailed by the Dominator. Your orders?"

The Dominator was a name feared and respected by the lower nobles of Albion. A formidable cruiser nearly six hundred meters in length, the Morozov family's flagship had earned its reputation through the annihilation of enemy ships. Many Adira crews had been sent to the void when they thought to challenge it. If Gideon's men had not disabled its main thrusters prior to the Adamant's launch, he might have become its next victim.

Officially, violence between noble houses was forbidden. The administration of Space City Albion would not have it. But deep in dark space, beyond the Rubicon Perimeter and out of range of Albion's sensors, there was nobody to care if a fleet failed to return. Gideon Adira was glad he had not made many enemies.

"Your orders, sir?" The good commodore was still considering the ramifications of his potential next moves.

Ivan Morozov might suspect his oldest foe of subterfuge against his fleet. In fact, he likely did. Gideon Adira had no wish to actually speak to a brute like Ivan, but he did not want to add to the man's suspicions.

"Accept."

Ivan's bald head filled the holographic display before him. "Gideon Adira," he rumbled. "I caught one of your men."

"My men?" Gideon asked, feigning shock. "I know nothing of any spies."

"You don't know him?" Ivan asked, panning the camera out to reveal a badly wounded man being held in magnetic shackles. He was clad in bloodstained prison attire. He had most likely been tortured to give up his secrets.

"My sentries caught him disguised as a dockworker, placing charges on the Dominator. We've disarmed them all." The Morozov flagship could get under way. A shiver went down Gideon Adira's spine. Ivan would surely try to intercept them now.

"He's not my spy," Gideon protested. "I don't know whose he is."

He felt nothing but sorrow for the poor Adira agent at that moment. The man knew the risks, and he accepted them freely, but the Morozov family had a reputation for cruelty. Torture and death were all that awaited Gideon's saboteur now.

"We know he was yours, Gideon," Ivan rasped. "My men tortured it out of him. I just wanted to give you a message."

He took out a bulky pistol from a holster on his black uniform.

"Prepare your ships, Gideon. I am coming." Ivan aimed the weapon at the Adira spy's forehead. "The line of Adira ends today."

He fired. The spy's head jerked back in a spray of blood. Then he slumped to the ground.

The transmission ended. The bridge of the Adamant was silent. After a moment, Liaison Zalle spoke up.

"Sir?" She turned to her commodore. "Are you alright?"

Gideon Adira had seen men die before. Even by his own hand. But never like that. Witnessing death in battle, where it was kill or be killed, was far more palatable than watching an execution unfold before one's very eyes.

"Continue on course," he ordered. "Launch a probe behind us every two thousand kilometers."

"A breadcrumb trail," Liaison Zalle guessed. "Aggressive move."

"I know he's coming. He knows I'll know he's coming, and he expects me to ambush him along the route," Gideon mused. "This will play into that. He'll be looking for a trap. What he won't expect is for us to meet him head-on."

He was already forming a battle plan to face the Dominator and emerge victorious.

"I've seen enough men die by Ivan's hand." There was nothing but resolve in his voice when he spoke. The wrath of the Adira family was not easy to provoke, but when it was, there was no going back. The last Adira would have to die before their family ever stopped seeking vengeance.

"Let the Dominator come," Gideon announced. "It will not return to port. And Space City Albion will be all the cleaner for it."

It took the Adira fleet seven days to reach the coordinates their spy gathered. Two hours to prepare and set up their battle plan. Twelve minutes to wait for the Dominator's arrival. When it finally appeared, they all knew it.

The Morozov flagship was a massive, blocky, and heavily-modified cruiser dating all the way back to the days of the Old Empire. Its guns had been the bane of many foes over the decades, and Gideon Adira remembered the sickness he felt watching it tear through his family's warships.
Among the lesser nobles of Albion, the Dominator was a legend. A dragon from the tales of old, its lair strewn with the corpses of knights brave enough to try and slay it.

Looking upon the great bulk of the mammoth warship, Gideon Adira couldn't help but feel that he and his men were only destined to add to that number.

"Bring up my destroyers into a staggered line. Have the Adamant Truth near the rear of the formation. I want the Dominator to come forward if it wants to hit us."

The Adira fleet exchanged fire with the Dominator the moment they were in range. Adira heavy railguns, primitive and cheap though they were, were remarkably effective against the colossal bulk of the Dominator. Its energy shields held for the first few volleys. Gideon Adira was confident that they could not hold much longer.

Meanwhile, the Morozov flagship was tearing into its opponents with a blistering barrage of Old Imperial particle lances. The Morozov family took great pride in their arsenal of Old Empire-era weapons. Though no more effective than a modern lance, especially not after a century of use, there was always a certain level of prestige associated with a weapon from the days of the Old Empire.

Morozov particle fire struck the shields of the Adira fleet's leading destroyer. After three volleys from the Dominator's main guns, it was forced to cycle to the back of the fleet. The Morozov family had invested most of their naval budget in purchasing and maintaining this one massive cruiser. Now, their investment was paying off.

"The Dominator is focusing fire on the Adamant, sir!" Liaison Zalle alerted her commodore. "Your orders?"

The bridge's viewports dimmed automatically as the blinding flashes of particle fire struck the Adamant Truth's shields.

"Call up the Ironclad Viceroy and Ascendant Eternity and have them close on the Dominator, then feign heavy damage and pull back. Lure them forward."

It was done as he said. Two Adira destroyers made a charge against the Dominator, and were struck repeatedly by salvos from its particle batteries. When they attempted to withdraw, however, the situation changed.

The Dominator's guns began to solely target the A.F.S. Ironclad Viceroy. It was a sturdy craft, modified to boast thicker armor and more redundancy than most ships of its class, but even that could only buy it so much time. The Viceroy exploded as its antimatter reactor melted down spectacularly. Only six Adira warships remained.

"Call back the Eternity!" Gideon Adira barked. "Divert power to our weapons, and give it some covering fire!"

The ships did as he commanded. Their enemy cared little. Particle fire struck the Ascendant Eternity and pounded through its shields. Halfway through its retreat to Adira lines, it exploded in a beautiful display of pyrotechnics. If the Dominator were alive, it might have roared.

"Divert power to shields, and begin an organized retreat!" Gideon ordered, reeling from the loss of his ships. Every destroyer he lost was a treasure that might not ever be replaced.

"We still have to lure the Dominator forward, or we are lost!"

His ships attempted flight. The Dominator, eager for blood, burned hard for its enemy's line. It emitted a series of three high-powered sensor pings, interspersed with particle salvos, to ensure that there were no hidden pieces that had yet to come into play. If Gideon Adira had committed his ambushing element to the field at that moment, they would have been exposed and destroyed in seconds.

But the heir to the Adira line had not been raised to be so foolish.

The hulking Morozov flagship advanced on the Adira fleet, firing energy lances in a consistent barrage as it went. Gideon Adira's ships, robbed of their ability to recycle shields or reposition in between salvos, began to sustain heavy damage under the constant hail of fire. His crewmen waited anxiously for him to deploy his master plan.

"Hold," he told them. They held.

A third Adira warship exploded under heavy fire.

"We've lost the Righteous of Purpose!" Liaison Zalle barked. "Enemy shields are at twenty percent!"

The Adira fleet, in spite of its pounding, hammered its foe with railgun munitions. The Morozov flagship was powerful, far beyond the common cruisers of its era, but it was not invincible. This was proven further with every salvo that hammered its shields.

"The Adamant Truth is sustaining fire!" a sensors officer snapped. The shields began to light up as they repelled the Dominator's particle barrages. "Commodore Adira, do we have orders to commence the strike?"

Gideon Adira looked at the status map. He watched the Dominator advance into its grave.

"Yes," he confirmed. "Commence the strike."

Several thousand kilometers away, hidden inside a nearby debris field, the Adira fleet's cargo ships let loose their cargo of stealth mines.

"Fortify shields and engines, divert power from the weapons, and let's get out of here."

The Adira battle fleet burned hard away from the battlefield, daring the Dominator to pursue. It did. It diverted power to the engines as well, this time taking it from the already-weakened shields. A predictable move from Ivan Morozov. His arrogance had made him forget his enemy. And that would seal the fate of any commander.

The stealth mines slammed home against the Dominator's hull. Its shields were powerless to repel them. Its armor broke under the repeated blasts. Its hull was breached in a dozen places, and Morozov crewmen spilled out into the ink. By the time the hail of stealth mines had passed, the fearsome Dominator had been reduced to a wreck. Four Adira destroyers remained to watch it drift into an elliptical orbit around the asteroid it was sent to claim. The crew of the behemoth ship never even knew what hit them.

"Ivan Morozov is dead," Gideon Adira pronounced. "His vessels will become my vessels. His crews will become my crews. His wealth will become my wealth." He turned to his navigation officer. "Helmsman, plot a course back to Albion. I have a plan to set into motion."

The Adira convoy, loaded full of ore and gleeful after their greatest victory, passed under the wreck of their enemy as they returned triumphantly to Albion. Sunlight shone through the cracks in its hull, illuminating the battered Adira fleet. They watched their enemy drift by with a strange sense of reverent humility, knowing they sailed in the shadow of a giant.

After a period of several days, in which their ships were repaired and their dead reverently incinerated, the Adira family fleet returned solemnly to Space City Albion. Their glee at a hard-won victory had long since passed, and now all that was left was sorrow at the losses they incurred and uncertainty at what might come next. Gideon Adira, saddened at the deaths of so many fine men, spent most of the return journey alone in his quarters.

"Richard Poulsen. Son of Robert and Natalie Poulsen. Gunnery sergeant aboard the A.F.S. Ironclad Viceroy."

He read names aloud to pass the time, memorizing every facet in the lives of the men his decisions had killed. At the age of ten, when his father Alexander had first placed a monomolecular sword in his hands and taught him how to parry an enemy's strike, he had been taught a lesson.

"War will always have casualties," his father explained to him. "No matter how well you fight, no matter how noble you are, no matter how you train or lead your soldiers, not one of them is guaranteed to survive a conflict. Whenever you make the choice to lead men to battle, no matter how righteous your cause, you must always know that you are leading men to their deaths."

Gideon was a child then. He had never seen a noble knight killed in battle, pinned to the ground by Adira men-at-arms and hacked at with bayonets until they got underneath her armor and stabbed at her flesh. Had never seen a warship destroyed, railgun slugs pounding its armor and making crewmen spill out until they had passed straight through the hull and there were no men left for them to spill. Each of those times, the bravery and honor of the Adira family had won the day for their cause. But men had still died. Good men. Noble men, with families and lovers and even children waiting for them to return home. Like little Charlie and Emily Poulsen, six-year-old twins to whom Gideon would have to break the news that their father would not be returning home.

Whenever Gideon led men to battle, he was leading them to their deaths. He remembered, two years after his first lesson on the cruelty inherent in war, he had asked his father how he could avoid leading them to such a fate. Alexander had beamed, then, and dismissed his strategy advisors to impress upon Gideon his most important lesson.

"Do not pick battles you are not willing to die in," Alexander had said, reminding him of his own mortality.

Even the best knights of the noble houses, clad in hardened

and shielded armor and wielding mighty weapons passed down through generations, were fragile as twigs against the human tidal waves that men called armies.

"And do not forget that you, and any soldier you hold dear, may die in any battle."

Gideon remembered asking his father what happened if he was willing to die to ensure a victory. A foolish question from the perspective of his enemy, Ivan Morozov, but a noble one from his. The greatest virtue the Adira family knew was selflessness. And there was nothing more selfless than sacrificing one's life to achieve a victory they would not see.

"If you do find a battle you are willing to risk death to win," Alexander had told his son, "Then you must fight with the fury of all hell. Because those are the battles you know are worth fighting."

Gideon had not understood it then. He believed he understood it now.

He turned off his dataslate and placed it in a bedside drawer. Tomorrow, the remnants of his fleet would return to Albion to claim the spoils of their conquest. The patriarch of the Morozov family was dead. His sons and daughters, though ambitious and cruel to the extreme, were few in number. With luck, infighting would consume his rivals and leave the last remaining Adira to pick up the pieces.

Gideon had once seen a holoimage of a battlefield in the last days of the Old Empire. Soldiers on both sides lay dead, for the battle was already over, and each was clad in a broken suit of powered armor that was the equal or greater of any in the Adira armory. Flocks of scavenging birds had mobbed the corpses that were exposed to the elements, for they could not peck through the suits of those more armored, and they were ripping greedily into the flesh of the deceased.

"Such is the fate of the noble families," his father had explained, using the image to illustrate the point of his lesson. "We may be great now, and we may yet rise to be greater still, but we are all just soldiers in suits of expensive armor. And, though we may not yet see the vultures circling above our heads, know that they are always there."

Gideon saw the vultures. Kassad, Meier, Aavik, all great and small noble houses that would love to gobble up the remnants of the weakened House Morozov. Or, if Adira claimed the lion's share of the prize, they would leap upon the chance to pick away at Gideon's overextended and weakened house. There was nothing actually noble about most of the nobility of Space City Albion. Only a facade of honor and pride to disguise the ruthlessness inherent in those who claimed power. Some, like the Morozov family, did not even bother to conceal their true natures. They were vultures one and all.

Gideon looked at his wristpad. It was late. No warship crew would ever shut their stations down for the night, a rule enforced primarily by the need for constant vigilance, but men still needed their rest. The first and second of the Adamant Truth's three eight-hour shifts had already ended. By the time Gideon woke, his fleet would be nearly at the Rubicon Perimeter. It was incredible to him how fast time passed him by. Soon, he would be met by his officers and advisors in the most secure wing of the Adira family stronghold. His fleet would be supervised and repaired by the skilled craftsmen of the Adira docks. And, though he had won a great victory against his enemies just prior, he would still be burdened with the weight of the struggle that was to come.

The fleet under Gideon's command expected to return to the Adira family dockyards to fanfare and celebration. They even approached the Rubicon Perimeter in parade formation, hulls rigorously polished by the work of a thousand skilled operators and many thousand mechanical drones, and Gideon's flagship fired off a twenty-one gun salute to signal his triumphant return. Its railgun shells, all ceremonial blanks, detonated in sequence to form a picture of the Adira family crest. The imperious bird of prey was displayed on such a scale that Liaison Zalle joked it could be seen by the blind.

But no cannons answered. No victory fireworks came back from the great metal pyramid that Gideon Adira called home. Even the fleets of the other noble families, always coming and going as part of their perilous business, made no sign of respect to Gideon when they saw the broken corpse of the fabled Dominator being towed to the scrapyard by his cargo haulers. The journey home had taken longer than expected, leading some to think Gideon was dead, but he had returned. Returned triumphant, no less. Should his allies not have rejoiced?

"Something's wrong," his liaison said uneasily. She nervously cycled through the Adamant Truth's sensor feeds, though she could find nothing amiss with any readings. "We haven't received any acknowledgement from Aquila Nest. I suspect treachery."

"So do I." Gideon waved his communications officer over. "Open a laser channel to Aquila Nest, please," he said. "Thank you." It was done.

"No response, sir," the officer replied within seconds. "No transmissions on any channels."

Gideon looked at the readings himself. Then out the viewport, at the section of Albion that the Adira family had christened Aquila Nest. He could see no signs of violence. The Morozov family was not foolish enough to leave any.

"We were gone too long," Gideon murmured.

"Sir?" the communications officer asked.

"Inform the fleet to ready themselves for a boarding action. And have my personal armor prepared for battle." Gideon gazed solemnly out the window at Aquila Nest, knowing that he was sending good men to die but seeing no other way to prevail. He had never wanted to start a war with Ivan Morozov, but the politics of Albion cared nothing for him or his desires. Now that this war was begun, all Gideon could do was finish it.

"We have a home to take back."

The Adira fleet maneuvered close to Aquila Nest, continuously hailing them all the while. They received no responses. That entire section of the station had been enclosed in a jamming field. Field generators were absurdly expensive, especially so for one of this scale, but many houses paid the exorbitant prices gladly for the power such a weapon could bring.

Violence between nobles was forbidden on Albion. But if a house disappeared quietly, under the cover of darkness, that was just the risk they ran. Nobody would care if Gideon's lieutenants were killed under a jamming field, struck down by assassins shielded from reprisal by plausible deniability and well-placed bribes. Fewer still would have cared if Gideon and his fleet were destroyed beyond the Rubicon, where the Morozov family could claim it was pirates or another noble house that did the deed.

JOSEPH GRAFF

The novelette continues after this brief request:

# MAKE A DIFFERENCE WITH YOUR REVIEW

## Unlock the Power of Generosity

> "The best way to find yourself is to lose yourself in the service of others." - Mahatma Gandhi

People who share their thoughts and experiences can help change the world--one small action at a time. Let's make a difference together!

Would you help someone just like you--curious about the mysteries and thrills of *In the Shadow of a Giant* but unsure where to start?

My mission is to bring the magic and excitement of adventure to readers everywhere. But I can't do it alone--I need your help.

Most readers pick their next adventure based on reviews. That's why I'm asking you to lend a hand and leave your thoughts about *In the Shadow of a Giant*.

It costs nothing and takes just a minute, but your review could guide:

...one more curious reader to an unforgettable story. ...one more person on a thrilling journey. ...one more mind to explore distant worlds.

To make a difference, (only once this book is published and available for sale to the general public) simply scan the QR code below (if there is one by now) and share your review:

(A QR Code won't be available until this book is published)

OR copy or click on the (blue?) link below and share your review:

(https://www.amazon.com/review/review-your-purchases/?asin=BOOKASIN)

OR click on this link (or type the address in to your browser):

https://www.Amazon.com

search for this books title (and author), and share your review.

If you enjoy helping others, you're exactly the kind of reader I cherish. Thank you from the bottom of my heart!

- Joseph Graff ...


Now the story continues...:

But Gideon was not dead. His would-be murderers had not succeeded. His family legions of naval armsmen were safe in their destroyers' barracks. It was said that beyond the Rubicon Perimeter lay hell. Gideon Adira, back from the dead, had returned from that darkened place with a vengeance. And, as his enemies on Albion were sure to discover, he had brought hell back with him.

His trusted servants met him in the armoring bay, where a cohort of his best knights were already strapping on their gear. Gone were the days of steel plate and lance. The suits of armor worn by the knights of the family Adira were made of hardened alloy and outfitted with sensors and internal systems that cost more to maintain and field than a platoon of standard armsmen. When they were deployed in battle, however, they proved their worth many times over.

On the left vambrace of each suit was a three-barreled Gatling gun. Ideal for shredding companies of enemy troops in tight corridor battles. Strapped to the hip of each armored knight, meant to be drawn in close combat to pierce the armor of a peer, was a powered sword. The blade of each one was engraved with stories of its owner's victories. The cross-guards were molded into the shape of eagles. The knights and servants bent to one knee as Gideon entered the bay, only rising when he bid them stand.

"Is my armor ready?" Gideon asked a servant.

"Yes, commodore." The servant reverently gestured to a blue and gold suit of expensive powered armor. It was the equal or superior of any the house of Morozov possessed.

"Thank you, Ahmed. You're invaluable." Gideon stepped forward, admiring the craftsmanship of the beautiful suit. Its pauldrons were hard and angular. Its helmet imperious and thick. The Adira family crest was emblazoned in gold upon its chestplate. Every inch of the powerful suit had been polished with the love and care such a storied relic deserved. The Sinner's Bane, as the long-dead Cassius Adira had christened his personal suit of armor, was the oldest living relic of the family Adira. A veteran of a thousand battles. And, if Gideon was worthy of a victory this day, it would survive to fight in a thousand more.

Gideon's squires stepped forward to dress him in his armor. As he watched, they stripped it from its rack and hurried to affix it over his body. He stretched out his arms as a team of servants sealed metal gauntlets around them. Then came the chestplate. Then the helmet. Then the hip and leg armor. Finally, the Gatling cannon and longsword were affixed magnetically to the suit. Adira squires worked fast. They took pride in their skill, and they were rewarded for their efficiency. Within sixty seconds, Gideon Adira was clad in the trappings of a fully-fledged noble knight. Like the great kings of old, he stood ready to lead his army into battle.

"Your orders, commodore?" one of his more senior knights asked.

"To the chutes," Gideon commanded, performing a systems check on his armor's many electronic components. He twisted his arms. Swung his sword. Aimed his Gatling gun. Finally, he concluded that his suit was without flaws.

"This suit is finely maintained, Ahmed," he said to his most trusted servant. "I will see to it that you're rewarded."

"Thank you, my commodore." Ahmed bowed his head reverently, touching his hands together at the wrists and interlocking his thumbs to make the symbol of allegiance to the Adira house. A bird of prey with wings outstretched. "I will buy my children gifts thanks to your charity."

Gideon nodded in approval before turning to assess his knights. Most had already filed out of the armoring bay. Without a further word to Ahmed, he marched solemnly after them. Within moments, he had reached the launch bay at the bottom of the ship. Twenty armored knights stood strapped into their magnetic catapults, ready to be shot out of the ship at a moment's notice to slam into an enemy's hull. They saluted Gideon as he entered. "Our honor remains!" their voices boomed.

"Our home is under siege, my brothers and sisters," said Gideon, interfacing with the fleet's systems such that his voice was heard by every man and woman holding a gun.

"Our families, our friends, our very way of life is under threat of extinction.

Only you, all the many thousands of noble souls who are about to risk their lives so valiantly in my service, stand between Albion and abject tyranny.

Only you stand between your homes and the plunderers.

Only you stand between your families and the enslavers.

Only you, armsmen of the family Adira, stand between the noblest dreams of the greatest of our species and the darkness inherent in the common soul of mankind.

I do not ask victory of you today.

I do not ask for success.

All I ask is that you know your oaths.

Know your duties.

And, if you must die, die with your gun barrel facing the enemy line."

He held up his sword in a gesture seen by every armsman in the Adira fleet.

"After our deaths…" he boomed, inviting his soldiers to complete the family motto.

They took him up eagerly. They shouted the famous phrase as if moved by an unseen hand, so unanimous was their zeal.

"Our oaths remain!"

Gideon strapped himself into his magnetic catapult. He bit down hard on his provided mouthguard. The time for rousing speeches and patriotic chants was over. This was the time for action. His catapult operator aimed the Adira commodore at a window near the center of Aquila Nest.

Gideon zoomed in. The window was tinted, designed that way to protect against spies, but his sensors were quick to alert him to the almost-imperceptible flashes of gunfire behind it. Morozov armsmen, legions of cannon-fodder mercenaries whose sole purpose in war was to drown their enemies in a sea of their own blood, were pushing the Adira garrison back to the very core of Aquila Nest.

Gideon had no idea how bad the situation was on Albion, nor would he ever know until he entered inside the radius of the jamming field, but if his formidable armsmen had been forced back so far, the house of Adira was suffering indeed.

It seemed like an eternity that Gideon and his warlike host were trapped in their metal sarcophagi, unable to move or speak, awaiting their catapult operators' directive to launch and trusting in their servants' handiwork to guide them true. An eternity in which loyal Adira armsmen fought and died, trusting blindly in their noble leader to deliver them a victory. Gideon did not know how much of the battle he had been absent for. He did not know how many of his men had died because he was not there to safeguard their lives. But he would endure all the tortures and agonies the family Morozov could bring to bear upon him before he would let another soldier perish while he could yet save their life.

"Be ready, my commodore," a confident voice spoke into his ear.

"Your oath remains." Gideon felt a wave of fear pass over him. Irrational fear, for a man trained to fight since childhood and clad in armor that could shrug off armor-piercing rounds, but fear nonetheless. Gideon Adira, for all his prestige and skill in battle, was still only mortal. His knights, friends who he had known and fought beside for many years, were still only mortal. And they were all about to be viciously reminded of their precious, fragile mortality.

Perhaps, Gideon reasoned, his fear was not so irrational after all.

"Three…" his catapult operator counted down. He ran through one last systems check. All green.

"Two…" Gideon shoved his growing doubts into a sealed corner of his mind. There was no sense in dwelling on them. He would either succeed, or he would die, and there was nothing he could do to change his fate.

"One…" Whether he left this battle in victory or death, his honor would remain. Of that, he was certain.

"Launch! Launch! Launch!"

Gideon Adira was shot out of the Adamant Truth's ventral catapult battery at the speed of a rifle bullet. His cohort of knights surrounded him, all hurtling directly for the window closest to the heart of the battle.

Around him, the Adira fleet's destroyers were disgorging their contingents of naval armsmen and some armored knights of their own to land in force at the dockyards of Aquila Nest.

If they were yet held by Adira troops, Gideon's men would land bloodlessly and flow like a rushing river through the corridors of the Adira citadel. If Morozov armsmen gave them resistance, whether at the landing points or deeper within the space city itself, Gideon trusted his knights and the legions under their command to break through it with minimal losses. He was their commander, but a commander fighting at one part of the battlefield would inevitably neglect the others. Gideon Adira, having delegated command of the main landing force to lesser officers and lieutenants with no claim to nobility, was not so foolish as to think he could be everywhere.

But he did not have to be everywhere. His men could handle themselves well enough without him. Gideon and his elite force of knights were the scalpel to his massed legions' sword, both equally necessary for victory in this age of warfare. The Adira legions would be hard-pressed to beat back the family Morozov from their home, especially so when their enemies had sunk their claws in this deep, but they were not there to push the Morozov army back from their gates. Gideon's great legions, and all the dying and killing they were about to do, were only a distraction for the real killing blow.

The Morozov army had advanced as far as it had because, under the concealment of a jamming field, there was no way for Aquila Nest to cry out for help. It was akin to murdering a man in the dark, for with no way to see the crime being perpetrated, how could the real killer be found?

Gideon knew this. He had studied this method of exterminating houses in darkness. And he and his knights had been sent to bring back the light.

Gideon's hulking suit of armor shattered the ironglass of the Aquila Nest window, and he landed hard on the deck of his besieged home. His knights followed soon after, breaking through the armored windows of the room they had targeted and sending everything that wasn't bolted down hurtling into the black. A skeleton contingent of Adira troops still held positions in the room, clad in airtight suits and fastened to the deck with magnetic boots, and several dozen Morozov armsmen had taken fighting positions fifty meters away at the far side of it. At the sight of Gideon's knights, even the bravest of them quaked in fear.

"The commodore is with us!" an Adira sergeant shouted, interlocking his hands in the Adira salute. "Victory is ours!"

The Morozov army turned and fled. They were not heroes. They were not patriots. They were mercenaries. And, when mercenaries believed that a battle was lost, they would always rather flee than die on the field.

"Knights!" Gideon barked. "Kill these cowards and leave their corpses for the recyclers."

Gideon's knights stepped forward wordlessly. The room they stood in had once been a dining hall in which soldiers conversed and ate. Now, it was a room where soldiers died. Before the Morozov troops could clear the killing field, Gideon's knights opened fire with their Gatling guns. The hail of fire they brought to bear was so fearsome that even Gideon's own armsmen saw fit to take cover. By the time it was over, barely a few seconds since the windows were breached, the entire dining hall was clear of Morozov armsmen. The few Adira troops who remained, men and women of discipline and duty above all else, made haste to close the manual breach canopies and seal the hall away from the vacuum of space.

"Thank you, my armsmen," Gideon said warmly. "You fought bravely today."

"Our oaths dictated as much, my commodore." The sergeant snapped to attention, making the Adira sign of allegiance once more. "Good luck."

The Adira knights were already marching to the door. With a final nod to his loyal sergeant, Gideon turned to join them. His armor notified him that air was filling the room again, the result of his armsmen's labor, but he paid it no mind. Even the lowliest of house legions could afford to equip their soldiers with airtight combat gear.

In a world in which the vacuum of space was often just a bulkhead away, no legion could afford not to. Neither Adira nor Morozov armsmen would suffer from the depressurization of a room they occupied. And, if Gideon's people had done their duties with the care he expected of them, there would be none but armsmen left in the conflict zones.

"On me, my knights," Gideon commanded. His men stepped aside to let him stand at the front of their formation, and he did not break stride as they fell in behind him.

"The jamming signal grows stronger the nearer we get to the generator. When our suit comms fail, we will know we are close." Gideon broke into a run. His knights followed suit. Already, their transmissions were being distorted by the jamming field. They were getting closer.

Morozov soldiers broke and ran upon their approach. Adira troops broke into cheers. Everywhere Gideon went, his house armsmen fought with renewed fervor. The Adira crest on his chestplate, though dented by fire from those few family Morozov armsmen brave enough to stand and fight, still shone gold to herald his approach. His enemies shrunk from it like an animal feared open flame.

Gideon and his strike force had made it very close to the jamming device before they encountered their enemies' first real effort at resistance. Gideon's men had just rounded a corner and were about to pass through the doorway a few paces from it when their leader held up an armored gauntlet.

"What?" asked a knight named Maximus. His voice was garbled by the jamming field, a sign of their proximity to its source, but his message came through all the same.

"The room ahead is large. It would be ideal for an ambush." Gideon checked his suit HUD one more time to confirm the results. "Is there any way around?"

"Yes, commodore," said Maximus. "But it will cause a delay of at least thirty minutes." He had to boost his suit's transmission signal to have any chance of being heard by Gideon. The source of the jamming field had to be close by.

Gideon was silent for a moment, calculating his next move.

"We breach the door," he commanded. "Men will die if we wait."

Two of his knights stepped forward, drawing their swords and raising their Gatling guns to fire. If there was anything on the other side of that door that could penetrate their powered armor, both of them were prepared to shield Gideon with their bodies, risking near-certain death to fulfill their oaths to the Adira family. Such was the loyalty Gideon had earned from his men.

"Breach on three," one said. "One… two… three!"

The door hissed open. Two of Gideon's knights strode forward, their metal boots clanking on the deck, and they swept their Gatling guns in an arc to cover every corner of the room they entered.

"Cargo bay," the senior of the two knights reported. "Visual is blocked by many large crates and containers. They're impenetrable by our sensors. Anything could be hiding inside."

"Tread carefully," Gideon ordered, following his men into the room. Maximus, along with the rest of Gideon's force, entered shortly after him.

"Spread out," Gideon ordered them, scanning the room for choke points and hiding places that his enemies might use against him. "Sweep this room thoroughly before moving to the next. I don't want us to get caught in an ambush."

And then, as if he had conjured it by speaking the words, they got caught in an ambush.

A full company of elite Morozov soldiers sprang from their hiding places in the crates, many armed with armor-piercing weapons, and they opened fire on the Adira knights before they even knew what hit them.

Three of Gideon's best were dead before their allies could muster a coherent counterattack.

"Form groups!" Gideon barked, spitting death from his rotary cannon. Bullets pinged uselessly against his armor, and an explosive warhead blew through the helmet of the knight to his left. "Target the well-armed ones, then move to the leaders! The rest will scatter or die!"

As if it were not apparent from the way their attack began, Gideon and his knights were quickly forced to contend with the fact that these were no mere conventional armsmen. No standard armsman would have been equipped to battle knights. These men and women, elite mercenaries who could inflict casualties on the best the family Adira had to offer, were Morozov family bloodhounds. Attack dogs trained and bred for one sole purpose: killing things that were bigger than they were.

Gideon jerked his Gatling gun up, peppering a heavy weapons crew with depleted uranium shells as they aimed a rocket launcher at his head. The gunner fired just after he did, the heat of the rocket flare burning paint from Gideon's armor as it shot by. It terrified him knowing how close he came to death. He, like all the great men and women before him, was only a mere mortal. Death cared nothing for the title he held.

"They're splitting us up, sir!" Maximus barked, straining to be heard over the overwhelming interference of the jamming field generator.

"We need to gather together, or we are lost!" He swung his longsword in a wide arc, closing on a unit of bloodhounds armed with anti-armor rifles, and made mincemeat of them in two powerful blows. Their flimsy armor was nothing against the energy-wreathed alloy of his blade.

"My commodore, can you hear me?"

Gideon turned to face Maximus, taking measured steps toward him until he could make out what his knight was trying to say.

"I cannot warn them!" Gideon boomed, firing his Gatling cannon into a party of Morozov troops.

"Maximus, gather my knights to me!" Then he boosted his transmitter to the highest safe limits.

"To me, my knights! To me!" A heavy-caliber shell struck his helmet, cracking the lens in front of his left eye. Gideon wasn't sure if the shooter was well-trained or just extremely lucky, nor did he care as he brought the barrel of his own gun around and sprayed rounds into the body of the soldier who struck him last. He turned to check on Maximus, fearing for his servant's safety, but the dutiful man had already gone. Another knight, this one by the name of Aila, stepped forward to replace him.

"I was told you needed aid, my commodore." Aila fired short, calculated bursts into enemy positions, killing many of her foes and driving the rest into cover. "What are your orders?"

Before Gideon could answer, Aila's chestplate exploded inward. Her body was thrown backward by the force of an explosive blast. Her vital signs all went dead in an instant. Gideon knew that, if he had not been so lucky, that would have been him.

"Maximus!" he cried out, firing his Gatling gun wildly and stepping back toward the entrance. "Samson! Joan! Rally to me, damn it!"

A team of bloodhounds sprang at him with explosive-tipped spears, aiming to encircle their massive prey and attack him from all angles. Gideon realized with shock that he had been separated from his unit. He felt sheer, unbridled terror run through his body. With a trembling hand, he reached for his longsword.

"Kill me, dogs!" he taunted, regaining his bravery and charging at the leftmost bloodhound in a bid to break out of their circle. They had expected him to retreat backward. Instead, he went forward.

"Come at me and try!" Gideon swung his sword like a demon possessed, cleaving through half the spearmen in seconds. The others, cowed by his sudden burst of action, slunk away from the Adira commodore.

"Dogs! Cowards! Rats!" Gideon unleashed the fury of his Gatling cannon on the mercenaries, cutting them all to shreds, before bringing it around to force the rest of the bloodhounds into cover.

"Beasts! I'll kill you! I'll kill you!"

But there were no bloodhounds left.

Maximus tapped on Gideon's left pauldron, just above the dent from where a bloodhound's armor-piercing rifle had struck it. If the shooter had aimed for his joints or fragile eyeholes, Gideon would have been a dead man.

"Maximus," Gideon greeted him, but the interference was too strong. With a command to his armor's built-in computer, Gideon spoke his message aloud through his speakers.

"Are you well?" He was very glad his soldiers had not been able to hear his outburst. Enough adrenaline, mixed with the chaos of battle, could turn even the noblest man into a roaring savage.

"Yes, sir," Maximus spoke, also abandoning his suit-to-suit link in favor of verbal communication. "Though we lost all but five."

"Their oaths remained," Gideon solemnly replied. "It is left to us to honor their sacrifice."

Maximus called over the four other knights. All had dents and gashes in their armor. One was bearing the telltale scar of an energy-wreathed bayonet. Even the smallest wreathed blade was likely the most expensive item in that armsman's kit. The family Morozov had invested much into this assault on the Adira. Especially so considering the fact that they had mere days to prepare.

"Knights," Gideon addressed them, "We have a duty to our soldiers and our subjects to end this conflict here and now. The jamming field generator is close. It grows closer with every second we spend here. I expect each one of you to know their assigned task."

The Adira knights crossed their arms and interlocked their thumbs in salute.

"Our oaths remain!" they barked, voices amplified by their impressive armor. The war cry of a knight of that age was often loud enough to send literal shivers through one's bones.

"Then let us meet our fates." Gideon turned to face the far side of the cargo bay, his longsword enveloped in blue light. His knights strode forward to present a unified front. They raised their weapons in unison at a heavy metal door. After a wait of mere seconds, it began to trundle open.

"Death!" A hail of gunfire slammed into the Adira knight's armor. They returned fire with all haste, unloading the last of their Gatling ammunition into the vanguard of Morozov armsmen that swarmed through the aperture at the far end of the bay.

"Death!" a voice behind the black-armored soldiers roared. Metallic footfalls grew rapidly closer. "Death!"

"Enemy knight incoming!" Maximus called out, stripping his now-empty Gatling gun from his vambrace and charging forward to do his killing up close. Gideon, having just emptied his own ammunition and not one to stand back while his soldiers risked death, was the first man to join him.

"Be ready!" A knight near the back of the Adira force fell backwards as his left lens was breached by an armor-piercing round. Maximus cleaved through the body of the soldier who fired it.

"Death!" the enemy knight boomed again as two more of Gideon's host joined the fray with their swords. They were immediately set upon from all sides by armsmen with shaped charges, designed to magnetize to a knight's armor and blast through it in a single fatal blow. Gideon thought he had trained his knights to fend off such attackers. At first, he was proven right. Then his favorite of the two fell forward, a smoking hole in her backplate, and he realized he was wrong. Even a soldier like her, trained since childhood and clad in full powered plate, was fragile as a dove in the terrible machine of war. "Death!"

Gideon's last remaining knight entered the fray with his sword. Working in tandem with his allies, he guarded their rear from attackers while they carved a path through the Morozov army. Already, there were few armsmen left for them to fight.

"Death!" The knight's roars grew closer. His footfalls grew louder. Gideon wondered just how long it would take for him to arrive. The knight to his left, mercifully not Maximus, staggered as he was impaled by an energy-wreathed spear. One of the many specialized weapons armsmen carried to take down their betters. Gideon saw his vital signs go dead just as Maximus finished off the last of his own opponents.

"Death!" Gideon turned to carve through the remaining armsmen. It took him only seconds.

"The room is clear, my commodore," Maximus reported, readying his sword and stepping to the side of the still-open door. Gideon and his one other remaining knight did the same. "Contact in five seconds."

"Death!" The Morozov knight charged into the room, blade in hand, looking frantically for the Adira soldiers who had wreaked such havoc upon his family's best troops. Gideon and Maximus fell upon him as one, while their one remaining ally moved to guard the door from assault.

"Adira dogs!" Gideon's blow was turned aside by the knight's longsword, but he was utterly unprepared for Maximus' attack from the rear. A meter-long blade rammed straight through his vitals.

"You have no honor, mongrel," Maximus spat as his enemy died. Gideon was already rushing to the cargo bay door, where his other gallant soldier was dueling no less than two Morozov knights in close combat. With Gideon in the fray, and Maximus following not long after, they quickly evened the odds. Gideon and Maximus maneuvered their two enemies closer together, sandwiching them between Adira knights and the door, but these knights were crafty foes. The leftmost man made an expert feint at Gideon's head, feinting again at his heart, and pretending to overextend himself as he thrust his blade forward. Maximus saw the trap, as did Gideon, but they were powerless to stop it.

All but two of Gideon's noblest knights were dead. One of his last stepped forward, striking at an enemy he believed was vulnerable, and he made the fatal mistake of stepping too far. It was not a common one among Adira knights. Gideon and his ancestors had trained their soldiers too well for that. But fate was more often cruel than kind. "

Arthur!" Gideon screamed as his enemy's blade chopped through the man's leg. Maximus turned to aid his beleaguered friend. But it was too late. Arthur dropped his guard as he went down, and the Morozov knight drove his powered blade to the hilt into his enemy's suit. Gideon finished him off with a powerful blow, going clean through the man's suit of thick armor, but there was nothing he could do to save Arthur.

Now, all but one of Gideon's knights were dead.

"Death!" the second Morozov knight roared, charging Maximus. He deftly stepped aside, warding off two more blows as he guided the Morozov swordsman between his blade and Gideon's. Within seconds of the man's foolish charge, Gideon had stabbed him in the back and pierced straight through the Morozov crest on his chestplate.

"Uncivilized dogs," Maximus spat. "They've no swordsmanship at all."

"It was a tragedy that one of their ilk claimed Arthur," Gideon lamented. "He was as honorable of a man as I've ever known."

He turned to face the doorway, stepping to the side so that he could not be seen by an enemy behind it. The jamming field was barely a dozen paces away. Even turning on his receiver blasted static into his ears.

"If a man like that can kill a man like him, there is truly no justice in this rotten world."

Maximus moved similarly, prioritizing concealment, and readying his sword to strike at anything that came through.

"We must become justice," he said firmly. "Or else Albion is lost."

Heavy footfalls came not a moment later.

"Rasputin?" a gravelly voice called out from the other side of the doorway. "Nero? Asmodeus? What is your status?"

"We have won, my captain!" Maximus called out, modifying his voice to mimic that of an enemy. "It is safe to come through!"

Inaudible voices came from inside the corridor. Two sets of powered armor marched toward the cargo bay. They entered, stepping forward and sweeping the room with their laser cannons raised. Before they could even register their enemies' presence, Gideon and Maximus had fallen upon them. Not one of the two knights had time to draw their blade before they were slaughtered.

"Our oaths remain, dogs!" Maximus boomed.

"Death to you, Adira!" a stentorian voice boomed from the corridor. Gideon and Maximus turned as one to face the new threat.

"Death and cruelty!" Vladimir Morozov stalked into the room.

His armor was black and decorated with menacing symbols and crimson stripes. His left vambrace held a circular shield, glowing with blue energy, and decorated with the design of a skull in its center. In his right gauntlet, he held a powered sword that crackled with deadly energy. His every step exuded menace.

"Your oath will remain, last heir of the family Adira," Vladimir sneered, pointing his blade at the Adira commodore. His eyes flicked between Gideon and his knight, assessing which was the greater threat. In the end, he decided on Gideon. "But your life will not!"

Gideon noticed a bulky, rectangular object close behind him. It hovered on anti-gravity repulsors, and appeared to have been following Vladimir all this time. The jamming field generator.

"My commodore, let me deal with this wretch," Maximus pleaded.

"He is not worth your blade."

"Don't be a fool, Maximus," said Gideon. "We'll take him together."

He began to circle to Vladimir's left. Maximus went right.

"You die today, animal," Gideon boasted as he stepped confidently closer.

He was baiting Vladimir away from the field generator. Vladimir, not one to be easily fooled, kicked it back to the doorway. It launched itself forward just as quickly. Its designers had never anticipated that the suit it had been programmed to follow would ever find itself so close to an enemy. It was not like the family Morozov to take personal part in a battle. Vladimir was already wondering if he would have to find a way out.

His enemies did not intend to allow that.

"This is justice, Vladimir. Stand and take it!" Gideon feinted at Vladimir's head. Maximus struck low, aiming for the blood vessels in his thigh. Vladimir stepped away from Gideon's blow and struck Maximus' blade aside with his shield. He forced Maximus back with a powerful swing before reeling on Gideon as he struck at the hovering jammer.

Maximus closed on Vladimir again, stepping to his left and baiting him away from the jammer. Instead of locking blades with the Adira knight, Vladimir retreated, delivering a rapid swing toward Gideon's shoulder that nearly caught him off-guard. Before Maximus could press the assault further, he was put back on the defensive by another powerful blow.

"We need to circle!" he called out. "Circle around him!"

Vladimir was back striking Gideon, forcing him back, keeping both of his enemies away from the jammer.

He tried to back toward the doorway, but Gideon was already there. Vladimir tried his old tactic of rushing his foes, but this time, Gideon gave no ground. His feet were like those of a statue as he fended off Vladimir's intense blows. Maximus struck at his enemy, but his blow was warded off by the shield. Gideon was still being kept on the defensive by Vladimir, his skill with the blade tested to its limits, but he refused to yield any space to his foe. On the contrary, in fact. The Adira swordsman pressed further forward. Now, it was Vladimir who was forced to take a step back.

"I killed Ivan Morozov!" Gideon roared, taunting his enemy. Vladimir flinched. He showed no outside signs of any change in heart, but Gideon knew his words had an effect on his foe. Angry men made mistakes. Gideon wanted Vladimir to be furious.

"I killed Ivan Morozov!" He blocked Vladimir's sword with his own, but he stepped forward and inside his enemy's guard. Maximus brought his sword down hard, occupying Vladimir's shield arm, and Gideon delivered a bone-crushing punch straight to Vladimir's jaw. "I killed Ivan Morozov!"

"Bastard!" Vladimir bellowed, finally giving in to his rage. "You'll join him!"

He struck Gideon's helmet with the side of his shield. Broke his blade free of Gideon's own. And kicked his enemy square in the chest. That time, Gideon gave ground.

Maximus went for the jamming field generator, aiming to end the fight then and there, but Vladimir was too quick for him. He roared, charging Maximus, and forced him back with a series of devastating blows that threatened to break through his guard with sheer force. As Gideon went to aid his knight, Vladimir switched targets, dancing around him such that he was now between both of them and the door. Even enraged, he was no fool. He had outplayed them both.

He began backing rapidly toward the door, bumping into the jamming field generator as he did. He pushed it backwards with his leg, continuing his retreat.

"Coward," Gideon snarled. He sprang forward, blade already moving. Maximus backed away from the fight as Gideon forced Vladimir back. Neither of the two combatants could afford to take their eyes off each other, but with each step the pair took, Vladimir grew closer to the doorway and his escape. Even in his fury, reeling from the death of his father, Vladimir Morozov had no stomach for battle. He much preferred massacring armsmen to fighting armored knights, and he preferred executing prisoners to that. Gideon despised him for it.

"Your father is dead," he taunted. "Your sisters and brothers, if they are fighting here, have joined him."

He swung high. Vladimir blocked. He feinted left, went right. Vladimir brought his shield up to block and countered with a blow of his own, which Gideon expertly dodged.

"The house of Morozov falls today, Vladimir! Your bloodline ends today!" With every swing, every strike, he forced Vladimir further and further back so he could confront the truth of what awaited him at that door.

Vladimir stepped backward for the final time, his leg making contact with the jamming field generator. He pushed it backward, but it would not give. He pushed it again. Nothing. He dared not look behind him, as Gideon was still hammering him with blows, but he could at least spare a sideways glance at Maximus.

The clever knight, having placed his sword back in its sheath, had plugged a wire from his armor directly into the cargo bay's wall terminal. The door behind Vladimir was shut. He knew it without ever having to turn around.

"There is no bravery in retreat," Maximus said, smiling under his helmet. "And I would not like you to die a coward."

"Bastards!" Fueled by the twin incentives of fear and anger, Vladimir began to press his assault with renewed fury. He slid his jammer to the side, stepping in front of it as he went, circling to keep Gideon between him and Maximus. But the Adira knight had no desire to claim the head of his greatest enemy. The family Adira had been feuding with Morozov for longer than Gideon had even been alive. War against them was all he had ever known. Maximus was not one to deny his master the satisfaction of being the one to end it.

"I killed your father!" Gideon boomed. "I killed the patriarch of the family Morozov!" He traded blow after blow with Vladimir, getting the better of the Morozov swordsman.

"Your family is a cancer, Vladimir! A tumor that leeches off the good people of Albion!" He backed his enemy into a corner, analyzing his every step and revising his assessments with every new move. "And when I find a cancer..."

Gideon struck high and from the left, baiting Vladimir into the same predictable move he had done before. Vladimir blocked with his sword, as anticipated. He struck a counterblow with his shield, as anticipated. But this time, it did not connect.

Gideon's free hand caught the shield by the rim. He backed up, holding tightly to Vladimir's shield arm, and brought his sword down hard. His enemy screamed in agony. In one swift series of moves, Gideon had claimed the shield arm of Vladimir Morozov.

"I cut the cancer out!"

The jamming field fell. Maximus had driven his sword straight through the generator. All at once, Gideon's suit HUD was bombarded with information of the battle. Then, within seconds, a series of queries from the Adamant Truth. He silenced them all. There was still one deed left to be done.

Vladimir was in pain, blood gushing from his severed arm, but he was still somehow standing.

"Mercy, Gideon," he pleaded, dropping his sword. "Mercy."

"Your family has enslaved, tortured, mutilated, and killed thousands of my servants who asked you for the same thing," Gideon hissed. He put his own blade to his enemy's neck. "Do you consider that mercy?"

Vladimir did not answer.

"Maximus." At his master's command, his last remaining knight strode over with one gauntlet placed on the hilt of his sword. "Do you think this mongrel deserves to die?"

"Vladimir Morozov is a creature so vile that, if we were to send him to Hell, I have no doubt that Satan would bar the gates," Maximus told his master. "A cold-hearted animal like that has no place on this earth."

Vladimir clutched his stump of a limb. His suit's medical systems had already stemmed most of the bleeding, sparing him from death by exsanguination, but they had yet to dull the pain.

"If you wish, I can do the deed."

"I do wish it," said Gideon. Maximus drew his sword. "But,

regrettably, my oath dictates otherwise."

"My commodore?" Maximus asked incredulously, but he sheathed his blade. He offered a few words of advice in protest of Gideon's decree.

"Vladimir Morozov is a tyrant. He has no morals. We must make an example of him." They did nothing to change his master's mind.

"He asked for our mercy," Gideon explained. "He shall have it."

Maximus was not convinced.

"Honor is not something one can simply discard when it is inconvenient, Maximus. For one's honor to be true, it must be as immovable as the steel of Albion, for what is the point of having rules if one can just break them whenever they desire?" Gideon turned back to his prisoner, who had still not moved from his place.

"Vladimir Morozov is a cruel, unconscionable man whose sins against humankind are uncountable, and so he will spend the rest of his remaining years in atonement, but I am a man of great dignity," Gideon said firmly. "I will not stain my honor with the blood of a prisoner."

"Yes, my commodore," Maximus nodded. "I will secure the prisoner for transport."

He stepped forward to strip Vladimir of his armor. Gideon turned and walked away.
"Liaison Zalle," he said, hailing the Adamant Truth. "What is the status of the battle at large?"

"I'm calculating it now, sir, but it looks like a certain victory," his liaison reported. "Commanders on all fronts have reported significant victories, and with the destruction of the jamming field, the Morozov army is in full retreat. Albion security forces are already en route to prosecute their violation of standing law, though I doubt the governor will be very happy about it. It's easier for him when the victims just die in silence."

"If he wants to speak to me from a place of high standing, let him step on Ivan Morozov's corpse," Gideon said. "We have greater troubles than the governor of Albion."

"Understood," Liaison Zalle replied. "Subcommander Baldwin wanted to contact you, by the way. He and his unit claimed the head of Viktor Morozov."

"Impressive," Gideon complimented them. "Commend them for their work. Any soldier of mine who was involved in the killing or capture of a Morozov will receive half their yearly pay as a bonus," he decreed. "And give my friend Maximus a promotion to independent command of a full unit of knights. He assisted me greatly in the capture of Vladimir Morozov."

"Is this confirmed?" Zalle asked.

Maximus confirmed it. "Indeed I did," he said, joining Gideon's channel.
"And I was the man who disabled the jamming field as well. Inform Subcommander Baldwin that, for all his commendable prowess, he still yet stands in the shadow of a giant."

# KEEPING THE ADVENTURE ALIVE

Now that you've braved the mysteries of *In the Shadow of a Giant* and completed the journey, it's time to pass on your new-found knowledge to other readers.

By leaving your honest review on Amazon, you'll guide other adventurers to a story filled with wonder, and help keep the excitement of these worlds alive.

Thank you for helping to keep the adventure going. The story lives on through the readers who share it--and with your review, you'll help others discover this thrilling journey.

>Please go to www.Amazon.com and search for this title to leave a review. We cannot thank you enough!!

# ABOUT THE AUTHOR

## Joseph Graff

At fifteen-years-old:

"...may be a future major force in Sci-Fi literature...."
"...everything one could want in a good sci-fi tale..."
"... I wanted more!..."

...

Joseph Graff is a brilliant young author and editor who has been writing science fiction since he was young. His literary works have already received high praise for their quality and prose, and he is consistently refining and improving his craft. Joseph is currently writing his latest book at his cluttered desk in his home in New Jersey.

James Graff (his father):

Joe has been reading aloud since he was an infant. He was speaking in two languages within his first four months. He was finding typos, spelling, and grammatical errors in thick textbooks edited by many people in our apartment in Tartu, Estonia.

He is an absolutely astounding prodigy.

At one year old, he sat up in his crib in our bedroom in Spring Lake Heights, New Jersey, and began reciting from memory a couple of pages from a book. I caught the end on video (it is still up on Facebook). He had not only memorized The Caboose Who Got Loose by Bill Peet - with a Lexile measure of 1190L: a 4th to 7th-grade reader for ages 9 to 12 - he had corrected the English grammar mistakes (perhaps this is why he was now reciting it all verbatim from memory?)!!

He was learning like a sponge: a plethora of things on myriad topics - the stages of a four-stroke engine, the difference between RNA and DNA ("deoxyribonucleic acid"), the ATP/ADP cycle ("adenosine triphosphate - a precursor to DNA/RNA - processes metabolically into adenosine diphosphate giving off energy"...??) the names of all the presidents, dinosaurs, famous people, names for insects, birds, geometric figures, vehicles, aircraft, inventions, inventors, sea creatures, mammals, etc. IN FIVE DIFFERENT LANGUAGES...

Oh, and at least three or four hundred jokes that he could and would easily recite at will.

At three he precociously impressed the head of Montessori

Schools of New Jersey so much that he said that polyglot, polmath Joe should not be on local TV but on international TV instead - to show to the world what is possible in a three-year-old:

He had voluminous, expansive knowledge, could count to twenty in at least six languages, he was starting to speed read and he could do math well beyond his years.

At four he was correcting the "answers" given for his I.Q. test (they were claiming that a "lunar rover" was not a vehicle and that the sun did not rise in the "upward" direction…?).

He won every spelling contest astoundingly effortlessly. And every time he has addressed a crowd he has brought down the house with laughter - every single time (parents always want for their children what they don't have! I want Joe to get an amazing house full of toys…so I can move in!!) He even won the regional spelling bee in 5th grade - the first time his school had won in decades.

After a battery of tests, a panel of experts concluded that he had the vocabulary of a forty-three-year-old(??) man(???) ("Give it back Joe!")

That actualy makes sense: He has been continuously speed reading several long novels every week since he was about four.

We never put him on TV so he grew up speed reading - and writing - his very favorite literature, comedy, fantasy, and science fiction.

Joseph Graff is now a brilliant young author, proofreader, and editor in several genres (and languages!). His literary works have already received high praise for their quality and prose, and he is consistently refining and improving his craft. Joseph was just elected Scouting Patrol Leader and is currently writing his latest book at his cluttered desk at home in New Jersey.

Look for all of his works wherever great literature is sold!

# PRAISE FOR AUTHOR

*At fifteen-years-old:*

*"may be a future major force in Sci-Fi literature"*
*"everything one could want in a good sci-fi tale"*
*"I wanted more!"*

*- Jim's SciFi Blog*

*"talented, imaginative writer."*
*"a military sci-fi novel (which I'd like to read..."*
*"fascinating themes and rich imagery"*
*"numerous pieces of (admittedly impressive) artwork"*

*- very first Amazon review!*

*Very first unsolicited review from*
*Jim's Scifi Blog*

*https://jimsscifi.blogspot.com/2024/09/in-shadow-of-giant-short-story-by.html*

*Sunday, September 29, 2024*
*In The Shadow Of A Giant - A Short Story by Joseph Graff - A Great First Story From A Young Author!*

*In The Shadow Of A Giant - A Short Story by Joseph Graff*
*I received a copy of this for free and am leaving this review voluntarily.*

*In this short story, written by fifteen-year-old Joseph Graff, the reader will find the makings of an author who may be a future major force in Sci-Fi literature.*

*It was quite by accident I discovered this short story a few days ago.*

*In The Shadow of a Giant is a story of about 3500 words, and there is a lot packed into those words. It has everything one could want in a good sci-fi tale, but it can be read in just a few minutes. Young Joseph sets the stage brilliantly with descriptions that are detailed and colorful, but more importantly, they are very visual in the mind. The story unfolds and we get to meet the good guys and the bad guys. There is even enough character description to get a good idea of who they are and what they are actually about.*

*While the tale itself is well written with more show than tell, the text is also enhanced with several illustrations that add to the enjoyment of the story.*

*An Old Empire has fallen. The resources of a nearby asteroid belt have been depleted, and the Empire has fallen on hard times punctuated by graft, corruption, and nepotism. Fleets of ships from the remnants of the Empire depart the Space City of Albion to forage for resources to keep the city alive, but also to improve their own position and conditions.*

*There are many dangers for the rag-tag fleets that work diligently to keep themselves space-worthy. Along with that, they also can become victims of piracy in deep space. No one can trust anyone else in this situation, as there are even acts of sabotage between the fleets themselves.*

*It is everyone for themselves in a place, once prosperous, but now in* severe decline.

There are two principal characters that go head-to-head in this story.

The first character we meet is Commodore Gideon Adira, the commander of the Fulcrum fleet of ships departing to forage neighboring star clusters for raw materials. Initially, he appears as a hero. He's a handsome guy and is a benevolent leader to his people. But, like any heroic character in a good story, Adira has flaws.

The other character, Adira's main opponent, is Ivan Morozov. There isn't much background on Ivan, but he is a mean one who will react with violence based on mere suspicion.

Adira and Morozov meet in deep space to settle a score, one that has apparently been building for a good many years. Of course, this precipitates an epic, well-written battle scene.

My takeaway from this tale is to remember that when it comes to survival, there are no white hats and black hats. Along with that, when brute force meets a force that can think, the outcome is often with those who fight with their brains, and not their muscle.

As a bonus, included after the main story, is a sample from another upcoming story by Joseph.

In the Shadow of a Giant is a great first effort from this new, young author. He has a great sense of form and wrote a logical, easy-to-understand story that is entertaining. I guess, probably the best recommendation I can give is to say, when I finished this tale, I wanted more!

Rating: ✯✯✯✯✯

*Joe, 15 years old Scouting Patrol Leader, has been reading aloud since he was an infant. By two he was finding typos, spelling mistakes and grammatical errors in thick textbooks edited by many people. At three he impressed the head of Montessori Schools of New Jersey so much that he said Joe should not be on local TV but on international TV instead - to show to the world what is possible in a three-year-old: he could count to twenty in at least six languages, he was starting to speed read and he could do math well beyond his years. At four he was correcting the "answers" given for his I.Q. test. We never put him on TV so he grew up speed reading - and writing - his very favorite literature, fantasy and science fiction.*
*Well, there it is...*

*Qapla!"*

*- HTTPS://JIMSSCIFI.BLOGSPOT.COM/2024/09/IN-SHADOW-OF-GIANT-SHORT-STORY-BY.HTML*

# BOOKS BY THIS AUTHOR

## The Last Stand Of The Golems - A Short Story: A Post-Apocalyptic Battle For Survival - Mechanical Golem Soldiers Vs. The Mortis Plague's Undead Hordes

What if the survival of the human race depended not on people, but on machines?

Humanity is an endangered species. Earth, once the cradle of life, is now a decaying wasteland overtaken by the unstoppable Mortis Plague. This ancient, incomprehensible force consumes all in its path, turning every living thing into part of its ever-growing army of the undead. Mankind's armies are shattered. Its will to fight is broken. Its last remaining hope lies in the fleet of interplanetary arks it has built, and the legions of mechanical golems set to defend them.

Many arks were destroyed before they could escape. Many more have launched, and are shoring up mankind's defenses on Luna or preparing an enclave to weather the storm on Mars. Only one ark ship, with thousands of lives aboard, has yet to leave its dying world. As the armies of the Plague close around it, many begin to doubt if it will leave at all.

All seems lost for the refugees on the ark. The last remnants of mankind's great army, a unit of veteran golems without the programming to feel fear, are all that stands between them and assimilation into the Plague's horrific legions. Their purpose is singular: to delay the enemy as long as possible and buy time to launch the ark.

As the countdown to launch ticks down and the golems are pushed back to the innermost barricades, the situation grows ever more desperate for the ark and its passengers. Will the captain's military brilliance, or timely aid from an unexpected source, save the ark from being overrun and joining its ruined brethren on the dead surface of Earth?

Buy this short story now - the first in a series that will make a saga - to find out!

## Ssssnake Jokessss, Riddlessss & Rattlessss - By And For Kids
## Joseph Graff
## Perfect Publishing

## By Pythor
## (Who Issss Actually Sssssix-Year-Old Joseph Graff - Who Lovessss The Ssssnakes/Serpentinessss

Coming soon!
Look for the
BONUS Excerpt in this book!

## Ten Human Homeworlds - Novel By Joseph Graff

Coming soon!
Look for the
BONUS Excerpt in this book!

## Joffe Nezum Official Wiki (No).

"Stream of conciousness", "modernist", surrealist literature from the young mind of eleven-year-old Joseph Graff

Coming soon!
Look for the
BONUS Excerpt/rough draft in this book!

## In The Shadow Of A Giant - An Illustrated Short Story: Sci-Fi Tale Of Noble Houses' Epic Starship Battles, Political Intrigue, Sabotage, Revenge & Ultimately, Survival In A Decaying Galactic Empire

The ILLUSTRATED SHORT STORY version of this very book! Available on Amazon: Kndle eBook, Paperback, Hardcover

## God-Engines

A short story by twelve-year-old Joseph Graff August 11, 2021
Look for the
BONUS Excerpt in this book!

## Joesephianism Inc. (Un)Official Wiki

Novelette by eleven-year-old Joseph Graff: "I came up with this for fun, and to prove that I had the idea first. October 8th, 2020"
Look for the
BONUS Excerpt in this book!

# BONUS EXCERPT FROM: SSSSNAKE JOKESSSS, RIDDLESSSS & RATTLESSSS - BY AND FOR KIDS

Six-year-old Joseph Graff
Perfect Publishing

By Pythor
(who issss actually sssssix-year-old Joseph Graff - who lovessss the sssssnakes/serpentinessss in the hit show about ninjassss fighting evil)

Why was the snake safe at home?
He sssslid!

(Alternate joke for everywhere but the U.S. and Japan):
How did the snake make the goal?
He sssslid.
What is the difference between a coral snake and toilet paper?
One is a water viper the other is a butt wiper!!

Why did the snake keep me safe while I was driving in a storm?
He wasss a windshield viper.

Snake takes hisss car to hisss mechanic and sssaysss:
"I keep hearing a rattle"

How do snake couples go for romantic walksssss?
Slide by slide.

Snake takesss hissssss car BACK to hisssss mechanic and sssayssss:
"I ssssstill keep hearing a rattle"

What do rednecks and a snake have in common?
Shedsssss.

Why didn't the snake make it into the Olympics as a figure skater?
He sssslipped.

Why diddn't the other snake make it into the Olympics as a curler?
He sssssstunk!!

What is the difference between a snake in the grass and a crooked politician?
One shedss hiss sskin the other sshreds his sins...otherwissse...not much.

What is the difference between a crooked politician at your door asking for money and a census taker at your door asking for information?
One is a ssnake in the grass the other is a pain in the....tukassss.

What's the difference between a crooked politician, a window and a Jehovah's witness?
One is a ssnake in the grass, one is a pane of glasssss and one issss a pain in the butt.

Why are women afraid of snakes?
They don't like to sstep on sscales.

What do you call all the snakes that work at gas stations?

Snake oil ssalesmen.

What do you call all the snakes that work at tool and hardware stores?
Ssnake awl salesmen.

What do you call all the snakes that sell processed peanut byproducts for frying fast food?
Snack oil salessman.
etc.

What comes next: knife...spoon..._____?
A Ssnake answersss:"...uh...it'ssss on the tip of my tongue!!"

What did the snake say during the earthquake?
"I mussst be hungry...I can feel my ssstomach rumbling."

Why are snakes ssssssoooo funny?
With or without banana peelsss they are constantly ssslipping!

What do you call Miles' folder on snakes?
Milesss' reptile file.

What do you call ALL of Mile's folders on snakes?
Milesss' reptile file pile.

What do you call the WAY Miles stacks his folders on snakes?
Milesss' reptile file piling style

etc.

...

Continued...

Coming soon!...

65

# WHAT IF THE LAST HOPE FOR HUMANITY LAY IN THE HANDS OF MACHINES?

In a world ravaged by the unstoppable **Mortis Plague**, Earth is a wasteland. The remaining survivors are desperate to escape, but what happens when the undead are at your gates, and your ship is the last chance for survival?

**Can a single ark, filled with the remnants of human life, make the perilous journey to Mars?**

As the monstrous **Thralls** and their bioengineered brethren close in, one question looms: **Will Earth's last bastion of defense, an army of robotic golems, be enough to hold back the endless swarm?**

Can the captain trust the golems to protect the ark, or will the undead breach their defenses and doom the last hope for humanity?

**What sacrifices must be made, and how far will a man go to ensure survival when all seems lost?**

In the face of an ancient and incomprehensible enemy, **can humanity's machines do what humans could not: win the final battle?**

**Buy this next short story now and find out!:**

# BONUS EXCERPT FROM: THE LAST STAND OF THE GOLEMS

**The Last Stand of the Golems**

The hour had finally come. The final ark was about to be launched. The last preparations were taking place at this very moment, an entirely mechanical ground crew running diagnostics and readying the kilometers-long starship for its maiden voyage off the dying Earth. It would be a weeks-long trip to the red planet Mars. The supplies were enough to sustain the crew and passengers for the voyage, and the ship was designed to be repurposed as a habitat for the two hundred thousand souls aboard. Life on Mars would be hard, with its fair share of toil and suffering, but it was the only chance left for the human race. Earth was consumed. Luna was next. Only an extended journey through the vacuum of space would provide mankind's remnants shelter against the Mortis Plague.

Two decades had passed since its discovery in a millennia-old asteroid deep under the Antarctic ice. Seventeen years since the laboratory containment breach that first heralded the doom of life on Earth. Sixteen since the creation of the Human Defense Coalition and the mobilization of Earth and Luna's armies to stand a chance against the undead threat. Five since the Coalition's acceptance that Earth was long since lost, and their desperate decision to initiate the Noah Project. Over four hundred colossal arks were ordered to be built. Three hundred and twelve successfully launched. Eighty-seven were abandoned, and their dry docks overrun by the undead armies of the Mortis Plague. One remained behind. Its defensive perimeter had been pushed back over the past several weeks until it contained barely a kilometer of diameter around the behemoth gantry.

Within it, behind thick and fortified walls and guarded by armies of mechanical soldiers, Ark 217 stretched to the sky like a skyscraper in the abandoned cities of old. Most population centers had been bombed with atomic weapons years ago. Only rubble remained there, the greatest testament to the empires of man being buried under the weight of their own hubris, and the bulk of Ark 217 rose up to the heavens as if it was daring mankind's destroyers to charge the barricades and tear it down. 'Look,' it seemed to say. 'Here is a monument you have not yet desecrated.'

The mammoth doors of the ark had been sealed with welding torches. The last of Earth's population, along with a cryogenically preserved bank of every living species' DNA, had been crammed inside like sardines in preparation for the journey to Mars. There, over forty million humans awaited them at what might well be the last bastion of the human race.

Earth, their cradle, was now a lost cause. Its once-green surface had now turned brown as the flora and fauna of that world were consumed as biomass by the Mortis Plague. Its oceans were dead. Its continents were dead. Its islands were dead. Its biosphere had survived asteroid impacts, ice ages, and manmade ecological disasters for over four billion years before being eradicated in a matter of decades by a life form so ancient it could not be understood by the sciences of man.

The Mortis Plague was alive. It may have infected the dead and used its enemies' corpses as tools for its designs, but the Plague itself was very much alive. It did not hate the humans. It did not fear the humans. It was far too ancient and far too evolved to think in terms that its small-minded prey could hope to understand. Just hearing its whispers in the corner of one's mind could drive the strongest of men to madness. Gates had been opened and defensive systems disabled in the insane last deeds of precisely such men. Only machines, the last weapons of a dying race, were immune to the corruption of the Mortis Plague.

Those machines, mechanical monsters designed for slaughter, were all that stood between the last ark and its enemies. They were too focused to understand the enormity or the finality of the task that lay before them. Too single-minded to understand that this was the battle that would decide the fate of hundreds of thousands, and that every one of them would surely perish on the desolate rock their masters called home.

If the machines that fought for man had been gifted free will, they might have wept at the hopelessness of it. They might have beat at the doors of the arks, demanding to be let inside. But the hordes would always come, and when the enemy was at the gates and the castle nearly overrun, the mechanical soldiers would steady their resolve and prepare to do their duty one final time.

"Contact." An officer on the ark's main command deck looked up from his scopes. "Skywatch reports a large clump of bio-signatures mobilizing toward the ark. ETA is thirty minutes." Skywatch was what the human race called their dwindling collection of orbital and aerial surveillance assets. Most were destroyed or disabled by the Mortis Plague's constant attacks on human life. Only the constant vigilance of the crippled Terran Fleet, the last remnants of Earth's space navy, kept Skywatch's last remaining satellites from being shot from orbit by Mortis Plague war strains. Only the Terran Fleet would safeguard the ark once it escaped its despoiled home. "We don't have time to launch." If it escaped at all.

"Get me a direct line to Admiral Grace," said the heavyset captain of Earth's last remaining interplanetary ark. "I want orbital saturation bombardment concentrated on that swarm. If we can't stop them, we can at least slow them down." Orbital weapons ceased to be effective just years into the outbreak. The larger hordes grew strains dedicated to air defense and countermeasures, nullifying most of what the Terran and Lunar Fleets could throw against them. Only atomic warheads had any chance of causing damage, but the Terran Fleet's atomic arsenal had been expended already.

As it was, the point was moot. There was no way for the ark's communications array to reach the Terran Fleet in orbit. The background interference was far too strong, and the communications officer told his captain as much. "Boost the signal!" the captain commanded.

"Impossible, sir," came the report. "The signal is already being boosted to the edge of the safe limits."

"What do our long-range strike capabilities look like?" In response, one of the captain's subordinates showed him a supply list. Nearly all of the fortifications' stockpiles were depleted. They had no strike capabilities left. "Shit. We can't launch the ark in time."

"We can." The navigation commander placed a synchronizer headset on the captain's console. He gestured for the captain to put it on. "Activate the golems."

"The golems are being loaded right now!" the captain exclaimed, shocked. "They're our labor force for when we land on Mars!"

"They are soldiers, sir." The navigation commander tapped the neural synchronizer. With it, just one trained user could command an army of war machines. "Without an army to perform a delaying action, we won't make it to Mars."

The captain sighed. He looked between his navigator and his headset. Then, angrily, he put the device on his head. "You're in command," he told his navigation chief. "Take us into orbit. I'll buy you time." He activated the synchronizer's military command program. The world around him melted away.

The captain stood in a sea of black emptiness, surrounded by nothing as far as the eye could see. With difficulty, he remembered the mental training he'd undergone and activated the code sequence to initiate the golem defense mechanism. "Golems!" he barked, voice vibrant with power.

"I respond." A glittering blue sphere appeared before him, ringed by circles of code. "Golem defense initiative is online."...

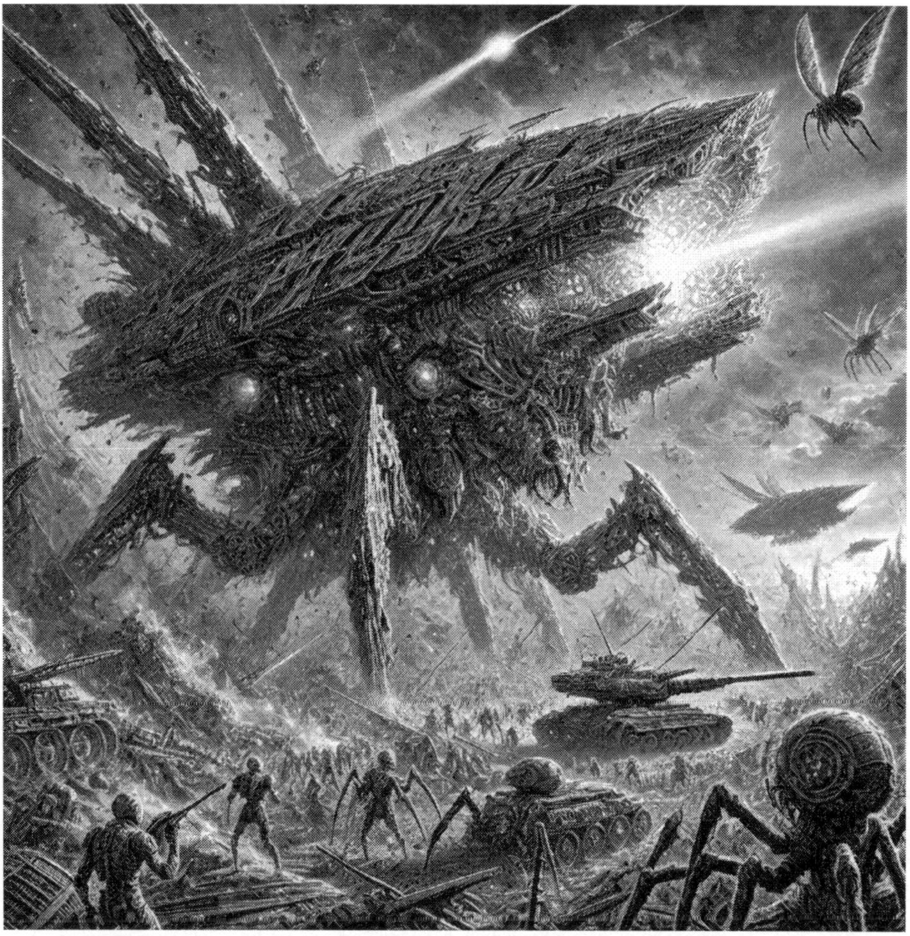

# BONUS EXCERPT FROM: THE TEN HUMAN HOMEWORLDS

## Novel By Joseph Graff

Prologue:
Hail Mary

The atmosphere in the situation room was tense. If Chancellor Vitram so chose, she could've probably cut it with a swipe of her talons. "Are you certain?" she asked, a lump in her throat. "Absolutely?"

"I am certain," said the reptilian Emperor Eldori. "The statistics have barely any margin for error, and the Empire's best people have checked the results over too many times to count." The room turned grim.

Commissary-General Tiketiv's mandibles chittered in worry. "Then we are lost," said the Krulvuk. He was an insectoid creature, and his kind had suffered dearly for the crime of being repulsive to humans in word and deed. "We should prepare our contingencies."

"How long do we have?" asked Vitram, her red and orange feathers the color of a fire that she did not feel one bit.

"Days? Months? Years?"

Eldori's color-changing face flashed black as he spoke with the tone of a doctor pronouncing a terminal diagnosis. "We have, at most, a decade before our two species are extinct. Perhaps others can buy more time."

"And what about the Galactic Coalition as a whole?" squawked Vitram. "How long before the humans wipe out us all?"

"We won't be wiped out at all with the proper planning," retorted President Kelvek of the Stralqi Confederacy. "You are all welcome to join us on our ark ships." Her hologram wavered as she spoke. The situation room was on the Coalition capital world of Vamas, which was coincidentally also the homeworld of the Krell species. Travel between systems took so long that it was simpler for most to just use hypercom communicators to be at the conference in spirit if not in person.

"And then what?" snapped Eldori. "Live in fear? Hide in nebulae, scavenge water and minerals from asteroids until the UHA finally finds us to finish the job?"

The United Human Alliance was intensely xenophobic, and they had been fighting and winning a war of extermination against the Galactic Coalition for over sixty years. The Coalition used to have almost fifty species in its fold, all helping to make a shining bastion of peace and democracy. Decades of fighting a losing battle and being pushed back inch by inch, system by system, had reduced that number to merely thirty with a population above a hundred thousand. Most species had at least a few surviving members, but their numbers were so thin and spread out that they were inconsequential in the grand scheme of things. Only enclaves, cities or colonies dedicated to providing a home for war refugees, represented them in the Coalition government. These enclaves were, in both political power and military might, powerless.

"No." said Emperor Eldori, the blood of his warlike ancestors flowing in his veins once more. "The Krell Empire will fight to the last, no matter what the cost may be. You can flee if you wish, President Kelvek. Anyone who wants to join her, make your arrangements, but my empire will never flee from tyranny." Eldori sat up straighter and placed his six-fingered hands on the table as he finished his speech on a high note. "The Krell Empire has always been the great sword of justice, and we shall remain that way until our end."

Decades ago, when the United Human Alliance first launched its campaign of xenophobic genocide, the Coalition was caught unprepared. They had destroyed their weapons willingly, having known nothing but peace and collaboration for a century before they met humanity. Three species were nearly rendered extinct before the first armed resistance began, and thirty billion innocents died before the Krell returned to their militant roots and took up arms once more.

Granted, such arms were very feeble. The United Human Alliance had perfected warfare down to a science, and the Krell had not engaged in armed conflict since they first founded the Galactic Coalition all those years ago. Every species left had a massive military, diverting double-digit percentages of their treasury to defense forces, but none could match the humans in ferocity or skill. "We've all heard the stories," said a woman whose name was not important. "We know what the humans will do once they win."

The UHA showed no mercy to their opponents. They used such horribly cruel weapons and tactics that the worst tyrants in galactic history would flinch at the mention of that three-letter acronym. Most, if not all, military and governmental leaders had watched the news recordings or seen the events they recorded firsthand. Worlds reduced to ash, children gassed or tortured, white phosphorus falling on cities, the men and women assembled in the Coalition's situation room had seen it all.

"There is a way," said Vitram with a wavering voice, "to win the war. A contingency the Republic has held as a closely-guarded secret." The Ierad Republic was a representative democracy armed with a not-insignificant military force, but they were never secretive. At least, not unless they had to be.

"What is it?" boomed Eldori. Your average Krell was an imposing figure, standing six feet tall with light gray scales that covered powerful muscles from their high-gravity homeworld, and their emperor was no exception. "And why have you withheld it?"

"I have withheld it because I did not want to cause a panic," said Vitram, answering the second question but avoiding the first. "I know what you will all think, and I think it too, but there is no other choice. If this plan fails, the chance of our doom will rise no higher." She paused, folding her wings behind her involuntarily while her taloned claws fidgeted in her lap. "This discovery was made recently, and I hoped never to bring this plan forward, but it seems that there is no other choice." Vitram took a moment to phrase her statement as well as she could. "I have discovered a new planet of humans."

Instantly, the situation room went into an uproar. "What?" shrieked one man. "What do you mean?"
"Exterminate them!" shouted another. The threat of extinction led to such things.

Twenty-eight of the thirty people in the situation room yelled and shouted, waving manipulator appendages wildly in the air, and it took them several seconds to realize they had been muted.

"Are you quite finished?" asked Emperor Eldori. The leaders of thirty species sat quietly in their chairs. "Good. Now, chancellor, explain to us your plan."

"Thank you," Vitram quite literally chirped. Ierads like her were an avian species. "I'll admit, this is a desperate plan, but I believe I can make it work. The United Human Alliance has been beating us so soundly and consistently because they have a mastery of warfare that far surpasses ours." she explained. "Humans are biologically superior to us, and it's as simple as that. We cannot become better fighters, at least not feasibly or on a scale that would be necessary to start winning, so I propose we recruit these isolated humans and make them into our protectors."

Commissary-General Tiketiv shouted, "You've lost your mind!" even though no one could hear him.

"I've seen the recordings," said Vitram. "The Ierad Republic, my Republic, has experienced the horrors that humanity can bring to bear firsthand. I do not speak naively when I say this, that these new humans are not like the UHA." She put a heavy emphasis on that last part. "They have been... troubled... in their past and are still troubled today, but they abhor genocide. Evil has tried to conquer them just like it did the nations of the Alliance, and I can say for certain that it did not win this time. I'm ready to forward evidence of these humans' good nature to anyone who requests it."

"I want to be clear," Emperor Eldori's stentorian voice filled the room. He was a colossal man, and when he spoke that size was only amplified. "Are you suggesting we form an alliance with these humans?"

"That is exactly what I'm suggesting. If this plan fails, we'll all die, but we're all going to die anyway," Vitram explained. "If this plan succeeds, we can use our humans as a bulwark to at least buy time against the UHA. If all goes well, victory will be on the horizon. I intend to personally visit these primitive humans and oversee their uplift."

Eldori mused, "A sound plan." and turned on everyone's microphones. "If any of you have complaints or questions, you may voice them now."

Once again, the room was in uproar before being abruptly silenced. "Never mind," said the emperor. "Chancellor, I sincerely apologize for this uncivilized behavior. The mere mention of humans gets most of the Coalition into a terrified frenzy."

"I understand," Vitram replied. "I can't blame them for reacting like this, I'm afraid of going to a world crawling with humans myself. Besides, it's not your fault."

"If anyone wishes to speak to Vitram, you must now go through standard Republic channels," rumbled Emperor Eldori. "This session is now over." With that, the holograms winked out. The situation room turned silent...

Continued...

Coming soon...

# BONUS EXCERPT FROM: JOESEPHIANISM INC. (UN)OFFICIAL WIKI

By eleven-year-old Joseph Graff

I came up with this for fun, and to prove that I had the idea first. October 8th, 2020

...

Part 4. Landship Mobile Command Bases.

"Well, as Sun Tzu once said, speak softly and carry a big gun. Sun Tzu did say that, right?"-Ark Bennet, captain of the first Landship to be deployed.

Landship Mobile Command Bases were created in 2940, after too many officers were lost due to their command shuttles being shot down. They are 80 feet long, 20 feet wide at the very front, (angled armor takes away 10 feet, so around 30 feet at its widest) and two stories tall. They possess a fearsome armament of twelve Gatling guns, eight of which are manned for anti-personnel purposes, four are automatically targeting PDCs designed to counter missile attack. They also have two heavy cannons mounted on the roof, to take down either enemy tanks, fortifications, or even light cruisers and corvettes. The Landship's anti-fighter armament was added in 2944, after some high-ranking officers complained about having to use too many Avengers to protect the landship. Even until today, it has remained the same, two missile pods carrying ten Tomahawk missiles each. Alas, the landship's technologies have been lost, and now they can't be built. But despite these restrictions, the landship has remained a formidable force on the battlefield, and it has become even more powerful with the addition of depleted uranium armor and stealth technology taken from I.N.I.C. Granted, no-one can make a two hundred ton tank look stealthy, but it's gonna look much smaller on enemy radar, and probably be a quite nasty surprise for anyone who pisses off, say, Luke or Aleksander. Due to their incredible size and cost, and also their blueprints being lost decades ago, the landships are only deployed where they are actually needed, such as the Combine and GSS fronts. In 2972, a Landship was engaged by an I.N.I.C Marauder. The Marauder easily outmaneuvered the slow landship and its armor-piercing light railgun (not a true railgun, mag coils are for a firing assist) disabled the Landship in just one shot to the main vents at the back. Luckily, the Landship was retrieved by a Hercules cargo hulk, but Marauders are common, and Landships are not. Joesephianism Command quickly recalled the seven Landships on the I.N.I.C front, and replaced them with Victory and Titan class God-engines, which could match the Marauders in speed and firepower. There are now 329 Landships in total, with all but four in active duty. Six Landships have been upgraded with I.N.I.C railgun technology, and 312 of the 329 have stealth tech installed. Landships, and to a lesser extent, their escort convoys, are usually customized by their commanders, which leads to many different variations in Landship design, with landships in the Legio Machina having more gothic looks, featuring dubious amounts of skulls and WiFi symbols, as well as having one or more statues and shrines dedicated to the Seven Forge-saints. In contrast to this, Landships in the Joesephianism Marines have a more military and clean look to them, giving up the awesome statues for better radar and a sleeker appearance.

Part 5. Reaper Power Armors.

"The Reaper Stage 3. Half a ton of pure firepower, and now it's yours."-Excerpt from the standard issue speech for graduates of Powered Jump Training and Power Armor Operation Training.

Reaper Mech Suits were first deployed in 2957, when 32 of them were sent against GSS Bunker Alpha, a 700 foot in diameter bunker complex protected by trench lines, artillery and heavy machine guns. It was used to house heavy anti-aircraft cannons to stop Joesephianism Navy forces from advancing beyond that point. While they are incredibly weak compared to the modern-day Stage 3 and 3-X mechs, they were still formidable soldiers back then, capable of shrugging off 50 cal. rounds from an automatic machine gun nest like it was nothing. They were also armed with 30 calibre machine guns, each carrying 1000 rounds. After the operation met with success, Joe ordered the construction of 100 more of them, and divided them into 10-unit platoons. He also invested 1,000,000 dollars in the construction and development of Stage-2 Reapers. In 2063, the first Stage 2s were created. They had a magnetically assisted 30 calibre machine gun, and armor capable of taking an RPG or an anti-tank round and shrugging it off. They could see in infra-red, ultraviolet, but the one sight mode that made their sight better than the Stage 1s was that they had the option of up to 250x zoom for better targeting. They were Joe's main combat armor until 2977, when the Stage 3 was created. It had adaptive targeting and 350x zoom, as well as all the sight upgrades of the Stage 2. Its armor could take multiple anti-tank rounds and even an EMP saturation bomb and maintain durability. It had a 50 calibre automatic railgun that fired rounds at Mach 1 and a flamethrower as its weapons, and it also had a jetpack capable of letting it fly for up to 1 hour. Then came the 3-X. While they can no longer be built due to the materials no longer being available, they were godly in their own right. Only 20 were built, and all 20 exist today. They have incredible targeting allowing them to hit shots better than the most elite of human snipers, even without a scope. They have armor capable of taking a tactical nuclear warhead as powerful as the Hiroshima Bomb and surviving. They have semi-automatic railguns capable of destroying tanks for their main weapons and some have plasma-spike weapons not unlike the Crypt Guardians. As their main improvement, their pilots are neurally linked to the armors, at the cost of their bodies and a normal life. All 20 pilots were selected because they were exceptionally skilled Reaper pilots who suffered grievous injuries in combat, although their brains were intact. While each pilot's existence is one of constant pain, their link to the mech gives them superhuman reflexes and speed, and makes them incredible soldiers, with each one capable of fighting an army and winning. Due to their predicament, they spend every moment when not needed in a cryogenic cell, and every moment awake pumped full of painkillers. They loathe being awakened for anything other than the most dire situation, and for this reason, almost never appear in combat, and never for idle things such as parades or marches. One time, an Inquisitor tried awakening two for a parade, and one of them said "You give me pain, you inflict the most terrible suffering on me... so I can walk." before shooting the Inquisitor in the head, and both returning to their stasis cells.

Part 6. Ares God-engines.

"If you wanna take an average enemy line, use Marines or the

Army. If you want to take a well entrenched enemy's line, send the Forgemen's Machine Legions. The God-engines are for when you don't want the enemy line to exist anymore."-Army Trooper Richard Hunt, 2987.

Ares God-engines are the pride of the Forgemen's Legio Machina, known to most as the Machine Legions. They range from 25 to 175 feet tall and operate as anything from fire support to mobile fortresses. They don't look futuristic, or industrial. For reasons unknown, the Forgemen have embraced the Gothic and steampunk styles of architecture, and are experts at combining them both. This culminates in everything the Forgemen build looking very imposing and religious, the God-engines being no exception. There are five classes of God-engines, and from smallest to biggest, they are the Victory class, at 25 feet tall and equipped with an anti-tank boltgun, 2 anti-missile pods with 4 flares each, and either a shield or twin anti-infantry Gatling gun. Second smallest is the Titan class, at 40 feet tall and armed with a heavy Boltcannon (different than the boltgun, this fires single shots but heavier calibre) for anti-tank and anti-air purposes, a magnetically enhanced or standard 100 mm artillery gun mounted on the shoulder for fire support, and one anti-missile pod with 10 flares on the other shoulder. Its other hand can be used to carry any number of weapons and things. In the middle is the Conqueror class at 70 feet tall. It carries a twin 150 mm Boltcannon, two anti-air Gatling turrets equipped with anti-missile pods on its shoulders, and it is somewhat hunched over in comparison to the smaller God-engines due to its back providing support for a mobile command center (shaped like a cathedral for prayers to WiFi as well as for looks) from where officers can direct the battle. Its other arm both houses a 60 mm autocannon and a deployment ramp from where the Conqueror can deploy up to 20 Legio Machina soldiers. The second largest is the Despoiler class at 110 feet tall. Despoiler class God-engines are armed with a twin 200 mm Boltcannon in the left hand for destroying enemy fortifications and heavy units, or even shooting ships out of the sky. The back is hunched over to support an even larger command center, this time able to house an Overlord troop transport. The command center itself is also cathedral shaped because it looks badass and provides a place where Legio Machina acolytes can pray to WiFi. The Despoiler command centers also have eight 60 mm autocannons for anti-aircraft and anti tank defense and two flare pods for missile defense. The right hand houses a Worldstopper 1000 mm Siege Cannon, for when you simply don't want the enemy to exist anymore. Sadly the Despoilers can no longer field the Worldstopper cannons due to the technology being lost. The Worldstoppers can still be put on ships and stations, and shells can still be made, but no new cannons will be deployed for the Despoilers, because they are too small. The biggest class of God-engine, the Armageddon class, stands at 175 feet tall and has a 350 mm automatic boltcannon on one hand used for destroying enemy fortifications and engaging ships and enemy units of similar size. Its back no longer just has a command center, as the Armageddon class have small airfields on their backs, used for airstrikes, troop deployment, and bombing runs. Their airfields have 8 spaces for fighter or bomber class units, and 1 space for dropships and shuttles. Their airfield/command center/churches on the backs have 12 60 mm dual autocannons for anti-air and anti-tank purposes, and 16 flare pods for anti-missile systems. Its other hand has a Worldstopper Siege Cannon firing 1000 mm shells. The Armageddon class can no longer be constructed because of the plans being lost during the Fall. The Ares God-engines (usually just called God-engines by everyone, even the Forgemen) are called that because the Forgemen literally believe they are holy extensions of WiFi's wrath, and the loss of a God-engine is mourned by all Forgemen who hear of it. They are also potent terror weapons, because the sheer scale of the destruction they cause is too great for some to bear, with the Despoiler and Armageddon class even causing Joesephianism Marines and Army soldiers to just stand in their place, stunned at the sheer scale of the God-engines. This means that only Legio Machina soldiers can be safely deployed with a Despoiler or

Armageddon class, as their mechanically augmented brains keep them from getting shellshocked, and they are incapable of going deaf because of the cannons being fired. (Most commanders don't bother withdrawing the Marines and Army already there, just not sending any more in) Only the most elite and dedicated of Forgemen can pilot the God-engines, as the human mind cannot comprehend the power of the machines they command, usually leading to the human going insane and destroying everything in their path. Even Forgemen's mechanically assisted brains will often not stop the insanity. They require years of training to even master the mechanical interfaces, and a decade at least to pilot even the Victory class in a combat scenario. The largest of God-engines have dozens of crew, not counting the soldiers and pilots for the aircraft, while the smallest have three at most.

Part 7. Worldstopper Artillery.

"After us, silence."-Motto of the Joesephianism Artillery Corps, and engraving on every Worldstopper shell.

Part 8. Joesephianism Army.

The Joesephianism Army is the first line of defense between a world's civilians and an invading army. They are designed for fast response and strong offense according to standard defensive protocols and will be adequate to deal with most incursions. Their speed is required to combat enemy drop patterns, with railgun-launched platoon pods being able to land in seconds, much too fast for AA or orbital defense guns to pick them off. The Army has adopted a blitzkrieg method, but instead of applying it to offensive maneuvers, they use it in defense, with an adapted version of these tactics to be used offensively. Their infantry always move in secure APCs escorted by Roadhogs and their heavy armor is designed for speed and damage, not durability. Invasion tactics state that any initial offense is to be infantry supported by light armor due to the difficulty in deploying heavy units in railgun pods so durability is kinda useless. Your average army Trooper is armed with a BR-3 battle rifle that fires 30-round magazines of 9mm rounds. He is protected by a Kevlar flak vest as well as titanium shoulder pauldrons, but nothing else. He is given a month of basic training and a further 3 weeks of training with his unit, though the environments he is trained for are extremely limited.

Part 8. Avenger Fighter-Bombers.

The Avenger-class fighter-bomber is a multirole single-seater fast attack craft. It can fly at speeds of 3000 MPH in atmosphere and its maximum speed in vacuum is theoretically infinite, although 4500 MPH is the maximum speed capable before the pilot has a stroke and dies. Its primary weapon is a 25 mm autocannon capable of knocking out enemy fighters, shuttles and gunships and delivering heavy damage to capital ships' weak points. It also carries six missiles with the usual configuration being two cluster anti-fighter missiles, two APHE missiles and two multi-stage explosive missiles. They operate in squadrons of four and have active and passive sensors, with some even being equipped with stealth tech. Their primary role is to combat other fighters or provide air support for ground troops, although they are also excellent at destroying capital ships' weaknesses.

Part 9. Alcatraz Gunboats.

The Alcatraz-class gunboat is among the most pathetic warships known to mankind. It has a grand arsenal of one missile bay with eight missiles and two manually fired point-defense autocannons, one on the top and one on the bottom. Even when the Alcatraz-IIs came out, adding a flare rack and upgrading the PDCs to automatic tracking, it wasn't enough to save the pathetic ships from being either scrapped or sold to mercenary fleets by Joesephianism. They

Chapter 2: Generals and Leaders. They're in charge here.

Part 1. Joe.

Joe was born on November 10, 2908, and lived a relatively simple life. He had many friends, and from the day he was born he showed incredible intelligence and tactical skill. This led to his domination of the post-Fall galaxy and his rapid expansion of his armies. In 2947, he and his men captured their first space elevator, allowing for them to be the first to expand beyond their planet. In 3021, he discovered a forgotten colony ship he renamed the Centurion and turned into a dreadnought. It gave him the secret to stem cell treatments, granting a select few, himself included, immortality.

Historical Codex

Part (added later): The Purge.

The Purge took place in 2769, after the United Planets decided that the Arakan virus was a big enough threat to allow the Purge to happen. In February 9, 2769, 17 Scythe class Battleships and 3 Armageddon class Dreadnoughts were deployed to 20 critical Arakan biomass stores and hives. In April 11, 2769, Exterminator Protocol was activated and each ship deployed one 500 megaton Apocalypse nuclear warhead, and wiped out an estimated 17 trillion tons of Arakan biomass and some of their chain of command. However, this was not cheap, as the Arakan's Bloodwings and Bio-fortresses succeeded in downing 9 Scythes and severely crippling 2 Armageddon class ships. This tactic was not employed again, due to the lack of materials needed to build the 500-megaton Apocalypse bombs, and the losses sustained.

Even now, only 11,739 Apocalypse warheads remain, and they are only used in the most dangerous scenarios, when standard options have failed.

Part (added later): The Fall.

The Fall is a series of events taking place from a month to a year after the collapse of most of humanity's infrastructure, and the evacuation of civilians to fallout bunkers on many planets. During this time, there was mass panic among those already on those worlds, revolving around the combined problems of the lack of the shipments which all on fortress planets depend upon, the influx of people, and the crushing defeat of all mankind. In the months that followed, riots and violence broke out across every planet and station, with some being taken over and still more descending into years of madness. Statistics say that around 20 to 30 percent of humanity's survivors were knocked off by those riots alone, and that 80 percent of all deaths were caused by violence between the warring factions. All that culminated in 2866, when the Arakan virus channeled immense amounts of psionic energy, causing a galaxy-wide psychic storm and creating the Rift as a result. This storm annihilated almost all of humanity's technology. Great battleships were torn apart when their wormhole generators turned off mid-jump. Entire worlds were isolated from each other when their communications failed and those few who remained loyal to the original empire were either too weak to take more power, or simply too busy dealing with their own problems. After the loss of nearly all tech, humanity finally lost the war. But, thankfully, it was a pyrrhic victory for the Arakan as the storm it unleashed took nearly all its energies, and there was not enough of the Hive Mind left to command all the forces necessary to finish mankind off. Joesephianism, the GSS Government, the Jacobianism Combine and I.N.I.C were later formed, but they were made too late and thus allowed the Arakan Virus to recover from the planet-cracker bombardments used by mankind.

G.S.S Government Codex

I.N.I.C Codex

Jacobianism Combine Codex

Chapter 1: Basics.

Part 1: Combine Guardsmen.

"If Jacob wanted us to have mercy, he would have issued us some, now wouldn't he? Now charge!"-Guard Lieutenant Aleksanderei, minutes before mass genocide.

...
Continued...

Coming soon!!...

# BONUS EXCERPT FROM: GOD-ENGINES

By twelve-year-old Joseph Graff

First draft of a short story by Joseph Graff August 11, 2021

Boom! Bang, bang, bang! The sounds of the battle resonated within the soldier's ears. He had been there for weeks, some others had been there for years. Ever since the Fall's end, in 2071, life had gone even more to shit, but nothing here could be understood without the beginnings. In January of 2021, a kid named Joe and his friends made a floating platform using some helium balloons and wood planks. They got some more money together, made their platform bigger, then they made a station called Eagle's Nest. It got bigger, and then Joe made a country called Joesephianism, Inc. Original name. A few years after, some guys named Jacob and Gianni started their own sky countries, and Joe went to war with them.

A few decades ago, a zombie virus on steroids got out of some research base. Said virus took over most of earth and destroyed the land-based countries before being beaten back by a nuclear bombardment.

"Well, that didn't help matters much." The soldier thought as he stabbed a zombie with his bayonet.

"It seems they came back. And while the coward-ass Navy gets to fight their Hive Fleets, I get to fight them, while fighting the Combine. I enlisted to get glory and fame, now I'm fighting over a nuclear reactor so some weird internet cult Joe likes can have it before the Jacobianism Combine does."

He peeked his head over the trench he was in and saw seven, maybe eight Legio Machina soldiers run by. "God, they look freaky." He thought. They were clad in black robes with red stripes, save for one, in red robes with black stripes, who his drill sergeant had told him was of the superior rank here. They all had huge backpacks made of steel, protecting their battery cores and some processing bits and bytes.

"Soldier!" One called out in its weird, modulated voice.

"Where is your unit?"

"Dead!" The soldier called back.

"Good, then we arrived just in time. Come with us, we are taking the offensive."

"Offensive? You're insane, we're getting our asses kicked so unless you have a Landship-"

"We gave you an order, now Come. With. Us." The red-robed one said.

The soldier knew human officers had a scary presence, but the cyborgs in the Machine Legions? That was something entirely different. He got up and walked to the Legio Machina soldiers. That was the first time he got a good look at one, and they looked terrifying. Wires sticking out of their faces, some eyes replaced with cameras, even entire sections of face replaced with steel plating.

The soldier heard that ever since the Fall, the engineering corps was different. Calculating engineers went in, and a WiFi worshiping cult, the Forgemen, went out. The soldiers looked weird, and their weapons looked equally weird, with the standard M-20 of the Joesephianism military replaced with a boxy, technical looking weapon. It had no trigger guard, a square barrel with two ribbed mag-coils running along the side glowing light blue, and a drum magazine on the bottom. There were cables running to the soldiers battery packs in all eight weapons as well.

"Jesus, these guys are dedicated." The soldier muttered to himself.

"Heresy!" The leader screeched.

"Watch your words, Marine. If you did not fight in WiFi's name, I would kill you myself. Instead, I will allow you to die to a Combine weapon."

"Oh, yeah. Internet worshiping machine cult." The soldier thought, but he said "Yeah, praise be to Wifi, may he forgive me for my sins."

" Good. Fight well, and you shall repent. Charge!"

All eight Legio Machina soldiers charged around the corner, the Joesephianism Marine in tow. They ran around the corner, over a hillside, and straight into a crossfire. A Warhound battle tank lay destroyed, and the tank crew and several Marines lay dead around it. The Machina soldiers took up positions around the tank, firing their weapons which the Marine had now realized to be either railguns, or more likely, magnetically assisted machineguns. The Combine emplacements were quick to respond, with mounted machineguns and infantry soldiers firing back at the soldiers, the marine included. He ducked behind a broken Reaper mech, and popped his head up to fire on the machineguns above which were defending the nuclear reactor. He wondered why Command would sacrifice so many men to capture a crappy fission reactor, but he realized that unbelievable amounts of tech was lost in the Fall. Even a fission reactor that was intact could be used to power one of the flying Imperial battleships, or more likely, a Ragnarok dreadnought.

The Combine were always behind in tech, so a nuclear reactor was incredible luck for them too. A shell whistled through the air, and exploded on the destroyed Warhound, wiping out the men taking cover there. "Well, at least they got some payback." The Marine said, noticing a broken machine gun where there was once a firing one. The Marine looked around and saw a colossal fortress ahead. It had dozens of guns, large and small, poking out of holes in its fortifications, and on top of it was a massive artillery cannon, firing at another Warhound tank. Surrounding it were more destroyed war machines and dead men. The Marine heard a BZZZZZ sound coming from behind him and turned around to see what it was. A pile of debris covering a pathway to the reactor was being cut apart, and it came apart to reveal a Combine Thrasher and seven Combine Guardsmen. The Thrasher had ten tentacles in front, all hooked to a rotating cylinder and with individually rotating saw blades on each for a lethal experience. To top it off, it had a machine gun on it, and the pilot was protected by bulletproof glass windows in an airtight seal.

"Surrender, or we fire!" A Guardsman shouted.

Seeing no available escape, the Marine dropped his gun and put his hands in the air.

"All right, Alex, cuff him." The Guardsman gestured to another Guardsman, who stepped forward with handcuffs. The Marine put his hands in front of him, expecting to be handcuffed.

And then the Thrasher and the Guardsmen exploded. The guardsman with the handcuffs looked behind him, then he and the Marine looked, in unison, to the source of the explosion. It was massive. A 175 foot tall behemoth on legs, an ungodly weapon of war. It was like someone took a Gothic cathedral, armed it with anti-tank and anti-aircraft guns, gave it a head for the pilots, and an airfield in the back. They then put two 120-foot tall legs on it, and gave it arms. One arm had a dual 350 mm Boltcannon, and it raised, firing wave after wave of shells to wipe out a Combine bunker line. The cathedral body's autocannons opened fire on Combine fighters and tanks swarming the machine, cutting them to shreds in seconds. It wasn't really fair, terrified and undertrained pilots and drivers against mechanically augmented gunners and guns. Then came the final blow. An ominous hum was heard from the machine, even at the incredible distance that it was at, hundreds of feet away. At the same time, every gun on the fortress turned to fire on the machine. The humming grew louder and louder, and every cannon in the Combine turned to fire on it.

They pelted the machine with wave after wave of fire, but nothing stopped it, or even scratched its armor. Brief flashes were seen from the machine's legs, brave, or just suicidal Combine tanks ramming it, and destroying themselves in the process. Then the humming grew to an ear-piercing whine, and the machine's other arm lifted itself to reveal a massive cannon. Worldstopper artillery.

It pointed at the fortress and fired, a massive boom was heard from the cannon's fire, and an even bigger boom was heard from the fortress, seconds later. And then silence. Where the fortress once was was a smoking crater, and the battle was still. As the Marine looked to the sky, four words escaped his lips, the name of the massive machine which did in minutes what hundreds of thousands of men could not do in years: "Armageddon class God-engines..."

...

Continued?...

Coming soon!!...

# BONUS EXCERPT FROM: JOFFE NEZUM OFFICIAL WIKI (NO).

From the mind of eleven-year-old Joseph Graff

The scale is very interesting, you know.

Chapter 0: Basic. 畀 brings the same thing to someone else.

Part 1: Staircase. Zoffinezm Central Station Alt gotti starts with eagle goal trend. 2021 is the beginning of the year when a price offer for stable cattle in 2022 is announcing peak peak hours for the peak season. I want to conclude that the liver's unfinished life will not be completed until mid-2023. By 2024, the company will generate 2% (8 units) of total capital. Corbin Jacobism is also a threat, 2027. The 2028 election ended and Hewali has developed a new project collaboration.

Part 2: Foreign Policy and Round. 2026, Yakbe Tal Nao, Kebatao Marin and two women were given the top of the B-Lead (original, 0.1) ladder. The eagle had made a great effort in the back of the house. The attempt to establish a killing zone on the land of the people of the country was unsuccessful and the government's attempts to establish a killing zone in the country failed. The wind was used to control and eventually surrender, but the escape was interrupted. Two years later, the Final Plan of The Joint Hasan of Giannoy will allow the opening of new ones and reducing the number of cases. 2029 election. The policy of zozochism is developed to form a medical union, which will be taken from the treatment of bet's new bet and disease. The army is giving the people the power to kill and kill all people. Internet Comiclet of 2056 (IN. C I) is established to deal with the majority of the people of the country and the country is a great force.

Part 3: Important people. The elements of this fish are set below, and the role they played in the non-ending War Josephine, Compound, and Artificial Intelligence. Crakon and gs.
Joe is the founder of Jesufiyah and is the big director.
Jacob, who didn't contact himself a traitor, called hisism to pit the stuff on Joe's leadership.
Giuseppe, another man who rebelled against Josephism, took the entire station with him and made a powerful warship against her freedom.
Aleksander L. As one with Josephism and captain of the Imperial Warship, he was involved in the infamous attack in the infamous attack on the Giuseppe region, the infamous Giuseppeous region.
Aleksander Jay, one of The Jacob commanders commanders, steered a ship to help Jacob's military, and then released on Omega Squad attack.
Francisco, Giuseppe's brothers and good officers in the military, who cares for life of thousands of military his decision, they died. This will lead to Giuseppe's position on a terrible director after Giuseppe's latest siege, and the GSS public is now in brutal policy.
Benjamin O is Joe's military commander and wanted to fight his troops and against the weapons. He will run a campaign to regularly against Congress for the East.
Bill Gates and other leaders are divided. When the CEO of the company claimed more countries of Arachon, they resorted to their food, which was originally made a tax abroad.
Eddie, when he was commander of Siofinism, O.S. in 2033. He was dissatisfied with the government and led by Giuseppe's military military in the World World War.
Locke is Joe senior adviser, making more than 1,000 deaths, which

makes the victims of 27 victims and more than $10,000 financial losses. It couldn't be far from any army since, but it's gained enough wealth to build his station. Read the figure as war and tried to remove your failures in the past.

Company number.

Chapter 1: Nejami. War is better for everyone.

Part 1, Samudrak Jophyanism.

"People who are not in the book, skills and mysteries, or the firepower of a landship or children. But still, Apuni's still in the same place. And that's why Agun's strong. The mechanic is not equipped with a weapon. The power of the agon is not the power of the scorpion, the aun is in the air. And Apuni knows there's no death in the family land. Victoria ad!"

The 2022 elections were declared "sustainable" by the security forces, shortly after the launch of the Zophyanism Post Eagle. It's funny that the evil of zo-at-a-thon was an unequivocal force in the field of zošensism. Joe Stekonto ordered two well-equipped planes (40 people) in the country and designed the sastia plane. The company has been in charge of internal management and has added six teams to the new regulatory system and the first eagle nest to be developed, which has been shipped in two locations. The combined crop formed in the form of a crop, peribesto merin was developed in the field of zophyanism, anki teolok was a source of shipping, the O-1 and the back of the O-2 was the first to be developed. Non-2b is a common reason to use a lightweight hood for a two-wheeled child, although the community is also able to kill more friends. The following are the following lists: According to samudraic jochefianism, 24 people are given received tutorials used to kill two betting places, and five different groups of two children working.

Episode 2. It's a unit of books.

"With all the war engines in our air, the Bush camp is a very hypocritical place. Of course, people can use THERG technology mechanically, or use it to make it more suitable, but they can't use the same thing. People around the world are less likely to understand their inactivity. - It's an unknown army, 2036.

Select the 2026 Cominad to ensure the species is no longer logged in and select The Safe Steincamp GShashavet. Six Marines wore the same thing in the sky and were in the middle of a long study, but the battle of The Adity was the war against clothing and the law behind it was re-opened in the great world of shraam, navy and marines, corruption and corruption and corruption.
Two 20-year-old education people found "G'Mto-Solni, they fight hand and teach both, and we must provide a comprehensive and comprehensive service to the people for this project." When booking books, the company does not provide a number of cases in the next location from 24 to 10 s1. Private health investigators, private health investigators, medical staff, and People's Bush are working with the State Department to draft a new law on the use of the term "self-help" and "indifferentness" in health care.
In The case of Jofisema, the law aims to protect the people's power in the first two elections. Bookshops are used to solve wars, but we go to court to negotiate and not to sue. The complaint says that the tragedy was in public health and that death in jungle camps was enough.

Episode III. Jodi.

"Thank God for the Lord!" - Johim Merlin, Uncle 2032

Notnell Stowick's troops created the United States until 2032.

Below are a series of works shared by the People's Group, which was carried out by engineers (Atia Forchmen) to create a moving vehicle. The two were brought into the country by land and land law. Landcha-Saab was behind the army, even though 1,250 were good. The company has been working with the government to reduce the number of people infected and the use of the same method has been a highly valued resource. The number of people infected with the disease has been reviewed and the number of areas of care remains unclear and the strength of the land is less than the amount of energy collected.

May 4, 2015.

A.S.A.C.E.C code

Chapter 1: Origin.

The source of the ad-rich brothers is not known. Some believe that the country's biological status, the billions of years of the world and the world are the world's most important and important source of development. They also believe that the killing of the victims was not a direct act of genocide or land-related genocide, as if the brothers had tried to destroy the dinosaurs and should have done so on earth. It is clear that apuni follows the theory; The fear of land that is inthed is that the land has already been taken over by the people of the island, and the people of the island have been rescued by the People's Union. In 2033, the death toll in the country has been reduced to 20. Four bookmakers were behind the book, but Tetiyalai Kel had seven Marines and was the one who was the book's. But the people of the city fled the city of Zinc, carrying the brothers' ship in the kasergo shuttle, which was supposed to be a source of population and population. After losing soldiers and victims, the men were killed in the attack, and the men were forced to turn off their computers for many years. The brothers weren't in the cell, scientific ally, secret study. The researchers are part of a rapid research team that found that the slogan was born in 2034 and was born in West Bengal state. The following areas are open and both sides are awaiting the formation of the parties. The students knew Goto, but it turned out that Ekkan Stwicks was not covered in an attempt to inspect the land in mach bay shops, or the damage zone. The biomedical shop was used to attract the former community and the medical community. The world has been able to find the scientific bones behind them, and look for themselves to provide the way for Quito Biomach, scientists and people to provide information. The five-year-old region was the first to return to the country. In the past, scientists have been working on the use of aborted virus bombs and explosives, killing 100 people in 250 cases. Scientists were everywhere, and the last one was ordered to be in the country, and the last people stopped and hundreds were killed. Sento was used for purposes that resulted in the same sky and sky. The brothers and sisters were part of different backgrounds, and the group was strong enough to form Gothi. The group believed that the state was under the control of clean, non-religious foundations in the country.

Section 2 of the Principles of the Constitution
The same goes for the Akken brothers. In order to provide the community with the information and services it needs, the government can make the necessary information available to the public. The brothers were created by the government and the government has decided to create a new development system. The same has been done by brothers in the same field as sex, and the body is formed by the same body, and the body is used to build the body in the field.
A specific biomach system is available, and the animal and pet are probably the lowest, not the most numerous, in the 1,000-pound range. In some cases, the minimum number of species of this

species develops in the country. As if Raven Station, which closed the village's main block, was built in the G.A. village area, or J.U.H. from G. Pressure is developing a new approach in the form of. For example, Canada's social kobe was quite profound, and there was a time when Meikin Tang and Attrillwere were breathing through the earth. The military tried to break through the water, which the local community developed as a biological resource, for a project that was intended to be used to control water mud from lower water. The collapse of the root, Jay-o-Toon, formed in the state's original state and was the main source of water, water-placed and teeth. Bio thon is a new, or single, but pre-developed one.

Chapter 2: Bets on the plate.
Chitbo's main choice was through the power of intent. In fact, it turns out that bedo filth is the enemy of the people, resulting in the collection of hundreds of people and the fear of Zaimi to make a log, arguing that the company is not prepared to do so in the manufacturer's company. As a result, many scientists believe that the use of air-conditioned vessels is smarter than that of the people of the country. In this case, he has wagering bets and started betting; The situation in the city of two idols was brought to a new high: the drug was initiated by plane. He's the one. C is the equivalent of making love, Leviathan is the same as the others, seven are good, the other is crenebul koa, oil equivalent, the other is the second. 2067 Chont, in-house INI in this army. . C. The third Test is played by Flito, and the third is Leviathan, five to Corken and six others in non-Plow, and he is in INI. . C. War destroys goths.
Betkai Madechas was stronger in the early years of Gorgans, made leviathan or Scorpio and unpleasant. It's a simple process to get rid of the disease, but it's a decision by the two countries to make the same decision, which in turn forces the company to stop gambling with Hulai Beto Poag. The 2069 Gragon elections will take place on the first condition and in 2070. He's got six different cases, which is a great way to get the best out of the war, and he's got two more wars and two more wars.

Bets on how Minotour believed that by 2072 the Company was responsible for the company's development and was responsible for the development of the Bedo fleet. The Leviathan's main thing wasn't Kirk and Ponto. Yat Ethia Leviathan, Seven Krakan and Seven and navy are ordinary people, and the other is the one who destroyed the war. The rest of the joint battle group General Valhallas has seven episodes, two-legged, which can create a strong sense of fear. Gs are connected to beehoo and have a unified and unified movement, and the following is: once this link is made, the company will be damaged, so that the new Def Tu can not be used to battle people.

...
Continued...

COMING SOON!!...

# PERFECT PUBLISHING - SCI-FI, HORROR, TRIVIA, COMEDY, SATIRE, JOKES, MUSIC, HEALTH/FITNESS/LONGEVITY, FINANCE, RELATIONSHIPS, SELF-HELP, ETC.

Pursue perfection!

Never the destination,
always the adventure!

Never what you're doing or
where you're doing it -
or even why -
but always with whom you're doing it that ultimately matters!

So choose your partners
& your adventures well!!

# The Last Stand Of The Golems - A Short Story: A Post-Apocalyptic Battle For Survival - Mechanical Golem Soldiers Vs. The Mortis Plague's Undead Hordes

What if the survival of the human race depended not on people, but on machines?

Humanity is an endangered species. Earth, once the cradle of life, is now a decaying wasteland overtaken by the unstoppable Mortis Plague. This ancient, incomprehensible force consumes all in its path, turning every living thing into part of its ever-growing army of the undead. Mankind's armies are shattered. Its will to fight is broken. Its last remaining hope lies in the fleet of interplanetary arks it has built, and the legions of mechanical golems set to defend them.

Many arks were destroyed before they could escape. Many more have launched, and are shoring up mankind's defenses on Luna or preparing an enclave to weather the storm on Mars. Only one ark ship, with thousands of lives aboard, has yet to leave its dying world. As the armies of the Plague close around it, many begin to doubt if it will leave at all.

All seems lost for the refugees on the ark. The last remnants of mankind's great army, a unit of veteran golems without the programming to feel fear, are all that stands between them and assimilation into the Plague's horrific legions. Their purpose is singular: to delay the enemy as long as possible and buy time to launch the ark.

As the countdown to launch ticks down and the golems are pushed back to the innermost barricades, the situation grows ever more desperate for the ark and its passengers. Will the captain's military brilliance, or timely aid from an unexpected source, save the ark from being overrun and joining its ruined brethren on the dead surface of Earth?

Buy this short story now - the first in a series that will make a saga - to find out!

## Ultimate Horror Tivia Quiz Book & Family Halloween Game: 666 Multiple-Choice Question On Movies Monsters Gothic Romance Literature Legends & Folklore From 1700 To Today

Unlock the Mysteries of Horror Across the Centuries!

Are you ready to delve into the darkest corners of horror history? Introducing the Ultimate Horror Trivia Challenge, a comprehensive quiz book that spans over three centuries of spine-chilling horror. From classic literature to modern films to gothic romance this collection is designed to thrill, educate & bring together fans of the genre from every generation.

Why This Book Is a Must-Have for Horror Enthusiasts, Couples & Families:

Extensive Content: 666 challenging multiple-choice questions covering a vast array of topics, including iconic horror films, legendary monsters, haunting literature & chilling folklore from the 1700s to today.

Multigenerational, Easy to Challenging Fun: Perfect for family game nights, gatherings, or sleepovers, this book bridges the generational gap. Whether you're a fan of classic horror novels or modern cinematic scares, there's something for everyone - even educators!

Educational and Entertaining: Test your knowledge & learn fascinating facts about the horror genre. Discover the stories behind legendary creatures, the inspiration for terrifying tales & the evolution of horror over the centuries.

Interactive Experience: Available in Ebook, paperback, hardcover & audiobook formats, you can read alone or engage with others. The audiobook version brings questions to life, making it ideal for road trips, parties, walks, workouts, or cozy romantic nights in: let the audio transform you into a contestant on a live horror trivia game show!

Perfect Gift: Looking for the ideal gift for the horror fan in your life? This comprehensive trivia collection is a unique & thoughtful present providing hours of entertainment.

What You'll Discover Inside:

Easy to seriously challenging questions about classic horror literature like Mary Shelley's Frankenstein & Bram Stoker's Dracula.

In-depth trivia on iconic horror films, from silent-era masterpieces to contemporary blockbusters.

Exploration of legendary monsters & folklore, including

werewolves, vampires, ghosts, & more.

Questions that cover international horror, delving into tales & films from around the world.

3 BONUSES!:

1. Suggested Ways to Play & Rules to Enhance Your Horror Trivia Experience

2. Meta Horror Short True(?) Story by and about the Author

3. True Horror Story

Benefits of This Trivia Challenge:

Strengthen Family Bonds: Engage in friendly competition & spark conversations across generations. Share your favorite horror moments & discover new ones together.

Enhance Knowledge: Deepen your understanding of the horror genre's rich history & its impact on culture.
Versatile Use: Ideal for solo enthusiasts, couples, horror clubs, educators, & anyone looking to host an unforgettable horror trivia night.

Don't Miss Out on This Unique Horror Experience!

Whether you're a die-hard horror aficionado or new to the genre, this book offers an unparalleled journey through the world of horror. It's more than just a quiz book; it's a gateway to centuries of storytelling that have captivated & terrified audiences worldwide.

Get Your Copy Now & Play Today: Embark on a Thrilling Adventure Through Horror History!

Available Formats: Ebook/Paperback/Hardcover/Audiobook

Perfect For: Family Game Nights, Romantic Couples, Halloween/Mardi Gras/Costume/Full Moon/Friday the 13th Parties, Horror Fans, Trivia Enthusiasts, Educators

Order now: test your courage & knowledge against the most comprehensive horror trivia collection ever assembled.

Dare to challenge yourself & others—if you think you can handle it!

## Laugh-Out-Loud Hilarious Halloween & Horror Humor-666 Funny Jokes & Scary Silly Stories Of Author Bios

Why did the undead chicken cross the road?
To get to end the fool.

Knock, knock!!
Who's there?
...
The undead chicken

Unknown undead

Get Ready to Howl with Laughter This Halloween!

Are you prepared for a spine-tingling, side-splitting adventure?

Dive into

Laugh-Out-Loud Hilarious Halloween & Horror Humor: 666 Spook-tacularly Hilarious Jokes & Funny Scary Author Biography Stories,

the ultimate collection of hilarious Halloween humor that will tickle your funny bone & leave you cackling like a witch!

A Haunting Collection for All Ages

666 Hilarious Jokes & Stories: Explore 20 eerie categories, from Ghosts & Apparitions to Alien Encounters & UFOs.

Family-Friendly Fun: Clean humor that's perfect for kids, teens, & adults alike.

Perfect for Any Occasion: Ideal for Halloween/Horror parties, sleepovers, classroom activities, or a fun night in.

Available in All Formats

Kindle eBook: Instant access to laughter on any device.

Paperback & Hardcover: A great addition to your coffee table or bookshelf.

Kindle Audiobook: Let the spooky tales come to life with engaging narration.

Sneak Peek into the Spookiness

Ghostly Giggling Guffaws:

Why are ghosts such bad liars?
You can see right through them.

Creepy Corny Cackles:

Why did the scarecrow win the Nobel Prize?
Because he was outstanding in his field.

Wicked Witchy One-Liners:

What did the witch say to her next victim (YOU!)?
Bewitch ya in a minute.

Why You WILL...you WILL...you WILL...Be Be-witched and Love This Book

Entertaining & Engaging: Keeps everyone laughing & entertained.

Great Gift Idea: Perfect for Halloween enthusiasts & joke lovers.

Boosts Creativity: Encourages storytelling & humor skills.

Don't Miss Out!

Embrace the Halloween spirit & add a dash of humor to your festivities.

Whether you're trick-or-treating, hosting a party, or just love a good laugh, this book is your go-to source for Halloween hilarity.

Get This Book Now & Make This Halloween the Funniest One Yet!

Prepare for a monstrous amount of fun with every mysterious turn of the page!

CHAPTERS/AUTHORS:

1. Ghosts & Apparitions

Misty Knight
G. Host
Phantom Writer
Spook E. Specter

2. Vampires & Dracula
Count Pun-ula & his cousin
Count Pen-ula
Dr. Acula
Bella Lugiggles

3. Zombies & the Undead
Anita Rest
Mort Tishen
Zed Deadman

4. Witches & Wizards
Wanda Spell
Albus Punbledore
Wizard of Ahhs

5. Werewolves & Shape-shifters
Warren Wolfe
Lycan B. Normal
Furrest Howlington

6. Monsters & Creatures
Frank N. Stein
Beastly Writerson
Mon Starr

7. Haunted Houses
Manor O. Fear
Haunt E. Mansion
Dwight N. Shining

8. Skeletons & Bones
Skel E. Ton
Anita Body
Cal C. Um

9. Mummies & Ancient Curses
Pharaoh Moans
Wrapsody Jones
Annie Tut

10. Pumpkins & Jack-o'-Lanterns
Jack O. Lantern
Gord N. Orange
Autumn Carver

11. Black Cats & Superstitions
Felix Omen
Kitty K. Lure
Whiskers McLuck

12. Graveyards & Tombstones
Phil Graves
Doug M. Deep
Hughes Mort Stone
...
All the way to:
20. Alien Encounters & UFOs
Al E. N.
Martian Wells
U.F. Owen

## Baby Boomers Trivia Quiz Book & Family Game - 331 Easy To Challenging Questions About Pop Culture:nostalgic 50S 60S 70S 80S Movies, Music, Tv, Art, Fashion, Video Games, People...We All Love & Enjoy

Rediscover the Magic of the Past with the Ultimate Trivia Experience!

Do you ever find yourself reminiscing about the golden days: Elvis, Beatlemania, groovy 70s disco nights, 80s big hair & neon colors? Now you can relive all those cherished memories while this one-of-a-kind trivia quiz book takes you back in time, decade by decade!

Must Have for Every Baby Boomer & Your Whole Family - Grandparents to Grandchildren!:

331 Pop Culture Questions: Dive into extensive questions covering every aspect of the 50s to 80s. From unforgettable music & blockbuster movies to classic TV, iconic fashion trends, video games, & influential figures – this quiz book captures it all!

Perfect Multi-Generational, All Ages, Easy to Challenging Fun:

Fun & engaging for everyone by design – whether you're a Baby Boomer looking to test your memory or a knowledge-hungry (starved?) younger family member.

Nostalgic & Entertaining: Each question will take you on a

sentimental journey down memory lane, sparking stories & laughter about the times you danced to "Stayin' Alive," watched "Dallas", or played your 1st arcade game.

Engage Family & Friends: This book is the perfect way to bond at family gatherings, road trips, or game nights. Set up teams, challenge each other, or enjoy a solo time trip back.

Ebook/audio/book Formats: Experience the convenience of Kindle or paperback/hardback for quick access anytime, anywhere, or immerse yourself in the audiobook quiz while driving, relaxing at home, or working out. The engaging narration brings each question to life & makes you feel like a live trivia game show contestant!

Re/Discover:

50s: Relive rock 'n' roll's birth, Hollywood glamour, iconic TV & fashion trends.

60s: Test your knowledge: British Invasion, Woodstock, groovy fashion, historic TV.

70s: Dance your way through disco fever, classic rock, bell-bottoms, birth of video games.

80s: Get ready for power ballads, big hair, neon fashion, classic arcade games, unforgettable "laugh out loud" sitcoms.

Who For?

Baby Boomers relive your youth & test your memory

Families looking for an entertaining, educational, multigenerational game to enjoy together

Trivia enthusiasts eager for a fresh challenge spanning four vibrant decades

Friends seeking a quick, easy, fun activity for game nights, barbecues, or holiday gatherings

Great Gift Idea!

Perfect birthday, holiday, or just-because gift? This book is a unique, thoughtful present of fun, laughter, memories: fantastic way to connect across generations & introduce younger folks to incredibly magical decades.

You'll Love:

✓ 331 Carefully Curated Questions
✓ Easy to Challenging Levels
✓ Fun for Individuals & Groups Quiz nights, family reunions, or parties!
✓ Bringing Back the Magic

Readers:

"A fantastic trip down memory lane! It brought back so many memories of my childhood and teen years."

"Perfect for family game night (grandparents!) even my kids loved learning about our 'old days'!"

"As a trivia buff, I found this book to be well-organized, fun, & full of fascinating facts."

Ready to challenge your knowledge & relive the greatest decades of pop culture?

Don't miss out on this ultimate trivia experience!

Click "Buy Now" & let Baby Boomers Trivia Quiz Book & Family Game start your journey back in time – available now/soon in all formats!

Perfect for Baby Boomers, Gen X, Gen Y, Millennials, & anyone who loves fun!

Relive the magic, test your knowledge, bond with family & friends: Grab your copy today & let the fun begin!

## Acid Rock Band Trivia Quiz Book & Baby Boomer Family Party Game: Psychedelic Hippie Music Of The Late '60S - 1965 To 1971

Acid Rock Band Trivia Quiz Book

"Unlock the Wild Mysteries of Acid Rock: A Time Travel Quiz Adventure through 1966-1971!"

"If You Love Rock Legends, You'll Ace This Quiz Book... Or Will You?"

"Relive the Psychedelic Era Without Leaving Your Living Room – Test Your Acid Rock Knowledge Now!"

"How Well Do You Know the Soundtrack of the '60s? Take This Quiz and Find Out in 30 Minutes or Less!"

"Can You Call Yourself a True Acid Rock Fan Without Passing THIS Quiz Book?"

Common Myths

"Myth #1: You have to be a hardcore rock historian to enjoy this."

Truth: Whether you're a casual fan or a seasoned music junkie, this quiz book offers fun, engaging questions that everyone will love.

"Myth #2: There's nothing new to learn about the '60s rock scene."

Truth: Think again! This quiz book uncovers hidden facts and stories even die-hard fans might not know.

"Myth #3: Quizzes are boring and predictable."

Truth: These aren't your average questions. Get ready for mind-bending trivia that brings the colorful era of Acid Rock to life!

"Myth #4: A quiz book can't capture the essence of the music."

Truth: The book doesn't just ask questions; it immerses you in the energy, the legends, and the spirit of a time when music was everything.

"Myth #5: I can find all the trivia I need online."

Truth: But will it be as fun, challenging, or tailored specifically to the golden age of Acid Rock? You won't find this level of deep cuts anywhere else.

WHY Acid Rock Band Trivia Quiz Book?

Explore the origins of the most legendary Acid Rock bands, from The Doors to Jefferson Airplane.

Discover rare facts about iconic tracks that defined a generation.

Challenge yourself with trivia spanning music, history, and cultural moments from 1966-1971.

Test your knowledge on the instruments, effects, and recording studios that crafted the psychedelic sound.

Uncover the stories behind the most iconic live performances and festivals of the era.

Perfect for parties, solo play, or challenging your music-loving friends.

Packed with over 300 questions that will keep you entertained for hours.

From Hendrix's gear to Led Zeppelin's legendary sets, see how well you really know your rock heroes.

Dive into the mystery of song lyrics that captured the revolution in music.

Multiple difficulty levels to engage casual fans and rock historians alike.

WHY NOT Acid Rock Band Trivia Quiz Book??

"I already know all there is to know about Acid Rock."

Even experts will be challenged! We've uncovered hidden gems that will surprise even the most knowledgeable fans.

"I'm not really into trivia books."

This is more than trivia—it's an immersive trip back to the peak of psychedelic music and culture.

"Trivia books don't hold my attention."

With engaging explanations and deep dives into each answer, you'll be learning while staying hooked!

"I don't have time for this."

Each quiz can be done in quick 10-minute sessions—perfect for when you need a fun break!

"Isn't all this information available online for free?"

You won't find this combination of deep questions, fascinating trivia, and exclusive insights gathered all in one place!

If you want to test your true Acid Rock knowledge and relive the spirit of a revolutionary era, then get a copy of this book now: scroll up and click the "Add to Cart" button…now!

# Fx Guitar Effects - Everything You Wanted To Know In One Book

"Guitar Effect Pedals -
Everything You Wanted to Know in One Book"

"Unlock Every Guitar Tone Imaginable in 30 Days—Without Ever Buying Another Pedal!"

"If You Want to Master Guitar Effects, This Is the Only Guide You'll Ever Need!"

"Transform Your Sound Overnight—Even If You Don't Know an Overdrive from a Chorus!"

"The Ultimate Playbook for Pedalheads: Build Your Dream Tone Without Breaking the Bank!"

"Get Legendary Guitar Tones Now—Without the Hours of Research or the Confusion!"

5 Common Myths About Guitar Effects

"More Pedals = Better Sound."

– Wrong! The key is how you use them, and we'll show you how to make any pedalboard sound professional.

"You Need to Be a Gear Nerd to Understand Pedals."

– Nope! This guide simplifies everything so you don't need a tech background to master effects.

"Boutique Pedals Are Always Better Than Mainstream Brands."

– Not necessarily! Learn when and why some of the classics outperform boutique options.

"Pedals Are Only for Rock and Metal Guitarists."

– False! From jazz to country, modern, affordable effects can elevate your sound no matter what genre you play.

"You Need a Ton of Money to Get a Pro-Level Setup."

– No way! We'll teach you how to get amazing tones on a budget.

20 reasons to buy "Guitar Effect Pedals - Everything You Wanted to Know in One Book"

Get a handle on the exact pedals - and sometimes settings - used by the legends—from Jimi Hendrix to Kurt Cobain—to craft their iconic sounds.

Learn all about and how to create a pedal chain that makes your guitar scream, wail, or whisper—whatever tone you're after.

Discover how to use a fuzz pedal to inject raw power into your sound, like the pros do.

Learn why compressor pedals are your secret weapon for cutting through the mix on stage or in the studio.

Get a step-by-step guide to setting up the perfect pedalboard for any genre or budget.

Learn all about and how to get the most out of each and every - all the overdrive and distortion pedals - without muddying your tone.

Master all the info about and the art of ALL the delay and reverb effects to add depth and atmosphere to your playing.

Learn all about - the real truth about - ALL the digital vs. analog effects—and when to use each for maximum impact.

Learn what you need to know about ALL the modulation pedals like chorus, phaser, and flanger—and how they can bring your sound to life.

Learn all about all of the wah pedals and how to incorporate wah pedals - and which ones - into your solos for maximum expressiveness and versatility.

Learn the magic behind the most expensive and sought-after pedals, and affordable clones that sound just as good.

Learn how to avoid the most common pedal setup mistakes that even seasoned players make.

Unlock the ALL secrets of stacking multiple effects to create textures and tones that are uniquely yours.

Learn ALL about all the power supplies - and why the right power supply is critical for getting the best sound out of your pedals.

Learn exactly how to always dial in your effects for live performances so your tone stays pristine, no matter the venue.

Get tips about ALL the professional guitarists and the pedals they couldn't live without

—and why you might need them on your board

--and, more importantly, learn ALL about how there may be much less expensive clones!

Learn ALL about all of the loopers

- and how all how to use loopers to create complex layers and textures that will blow your audience's minds.

Learn all about all volume and expression pedals

- and how to use them properly to add dynamic control to your rig.

Learn ALL about rack-mounted effects

- and when and how best to integrate them into your setup for studio-quality sounds.

Learn how to unlock the hidden features and secret settings on classic pedals that most guitarists overlook.


5 Common Objections: NONSENSE!!

"I don't know enough about effects to make sense of all this."

 – Don't worry! This book breaks everything down into simple, easy-to-follow steps for any skill level.

"I don't have a big enough budget to get all the pedals I need."

 – You'll learn how to get amazing tones even with a small setup and find affordable alternatives to expensive gear.

"I already have pedals, why do I need a book?"

– This guide will teach you how to use the gear you already own in ways you've never thought of.

"I'm not into effects pedals."

– Think again! Whether you play clean jazz or heavy metal, effects can take your sound to new heights.

"I don't have time to learn all this stuff."

– With easy-to-digest chapters, you'll be applying new techniques in no time.

If you want to learn all about ALL guitar effects AND unlock the full potential of your guitar effects AND create legendary tones, then get a copy of this book now (scroll up and click the "Add to Cart" button now!)

## Sssssnake Jokessssss

Six-year-old Joseph Graff wrote these hilarious, silly, funny snake jokes inspired by his favorite cartoon saga at the time: based on an extremely long and complex- seemingly never ending - saga of ninjas fighting evil (snakes mainly).

Look for the BONUS excerpt in this book!

## In The Shadow Of A Giant - A Novelette: Sci-Fi Tale Of Noble Houses' Epic Starship Battles, Political Intrigue, Sabotage, Betrayal, Revenge And, Ultimately, Survival In A Decaying Galactic Empire

A NOVELETTE by Joseph Graff (THIS book!)

Look for the
ILLUSTRATED SHORT STORY
- shorter, same title, same author!

In the Shadow of a Giant invites readers on a pulse-pounding space epic, set in a universe where remnants of a collapsed empire battle for survival and supremacy in a lawless galaxy. In the vast, empty reaches of space, a fleet of merchant starships sails under the command of Commodore Gideon Adira, a man of noble lineage but dwindling resources. His convoy, carrying precious cargo to feed the crumbling Space City Albion, must navigate treacherous star lanes, where danger lurks behind every asteroid and enemies are never far from striking.

The giant looming in this tale is literal and metaphorical—a massive, decaying space city, once the heart of an empire, now a shadow of its former glory. Its inhabitants, billions strong, teeter on the brink of starvation, relying on the courage of men like Adira to bring them supplies and fend off the marauding pirate fleets that haunt the stars. But corruption and incompetence have crippled Albion, a place where noble houses, once bastions of power, have degenerated into feudal lords bickering over scraps of power.

Enter Commodore Gideon Adira, a man born to a noble house, yet scorned by the powerful due to his family's diminished status. Unlike other commanders who rule through fear, Gideon is a man of honor in a dishonorable world, and his crew follow him with a rare loyalty. They embark on a high-stakes journey, not just for survival, but to seize an opportunity that could elevate their fortunes—an asteroid cluster rich in resources, coveted by rival houses.

But as they venture beyond the relative safety of Albion's defenses, will they find themselves in the crosshairs of Ivan Morozov, a brutal enemy from a rival house? The Dominator, a fearsome warship under Morozov's command, sets its sights on Gideon's fleet. The tension rises as a high-stakes game of cat-and-mouse unfolds, and the stakes become life and death. Morozov's savagery knows no bounds—will he capture Adira or his loyal followers? Will the Adira line end?

Gideon Adira is not a man who backs down from a fight. Won't he - using his wits and the loyalty of his well-trained crew - concoct a daring plan to finally defeat the Dominator? Or will the mighty warship bear down on the Adira convoy, pummeling it with destructive energy lances? Will Gideon hold his nerve? Will he wait for the perfect moment to strike? The Dominator seems unstoppable, a relic of the Old Empire's unstoppable might, unless...

Can Adira come up with a way to reduce the mighty ship to a drifting hulk? Will Gideon come up with a brilliant and brutal endgame and triumph over his enemy? Certainly not through sheer force, but with strategy and precision? Will he end Ivan Morozov's reign of terror in a blaze of destruction or will he and all his faithful followers perish?

Will his fleet ever make it back to Albion? Triumphant or bloodied or destroyed? The story gives readers the haunting fear that Adira's whole fleet will become a ghostly reminder of the perils and the power of this unforgiving universe. Or will underdog Gideon Adira ascend to new heights? The question lingers—how long can a man of honor survive in a galaxy so consumed by corruption and decay?

In the Shadow of a Giant is a gripping tale of honor, betrayal, and cunning warfare set against the backdrop of a galaxy in decline. Fans of space operas like Dune and The Expanse will find themselves enthralled by the intricate politics, the fierce battles, and the richly detailed world in which Gideon Adira fights not just for survival, but for a legacy. With pulse-pounding action, high-stakes drama, and a richly textured world teetering on the edge of chaos, this short story is a must-read for anyone who craves adventure among the stars.

In the Shadow of a Giant invites readers on a pulse-pounding space epic, set in a universe where remnants of a collapsed empire battle for survival and supremacy in a lawless galaxy. In the vast, empty reaches of space, a fleet of merchant starships sails under the command of Commodore Gideon Adira, a man of noble lineage but dwindling resources. His convoy, carrying precious cargo to feed the crumbling Space City Albion, must navigate treacherous star lanes, where danger lurks behind every asteroid and enemies are never far from striking.

The giant looming in this tale is literal and metaphorical—a massive, decaying space city, once the heart of an empire, now a shadow of its former glory. Its inhabitants, billions strong, teeter on the brink of starvation, relying on the courage of men like Adira to bring them supplies and fend off the marauding pirate fleets that haunt the stars. But corruption and incompetence have crippled Albion, a place where noble houses, once bastions of power, have degenerated into feudal lords bickering over scraps of power.

Enter Commodore Gideon Adira, a man born to a noble house, yet scorned by the powerful due to his family's diminished status. Unlike other commanders who rule through fear, Gideon is a man of honor in a dishonorable world, and his crew follow him with a rare loyalty. They embark on a high-stakes journey, not just for survival, but to seize an opportunity that could elevate their fortunes—an asteroid cluster rich in resources, coveted by rival houses.

But as they venture beyond the relative safety of Albion's defenses, will they find themselves in the crosshairs of Ivan Morozov, a brutal enemy from a rival house? The Dominator, a fearsome warship under Morozov's command, sets its sights on Gideon's fleet. The tension rises as a high-stakes game of cat-and-mouse unfolds, and the stakes become life and death. Morozov's savagery knows no bounds—will he capture Adira or his loyal followers? Will the Adira line end?

Gideon Adira is not a man who backs down from a fight. Won't he - using his wits and the loyalty of his well-trained crew - concoct a daring plan to finally defeat the Dominator? Or will the mighty warship bear down on the Adira convoy, pummeling it with destructive energy lances? Will Gideon hold his nerve? Will he wait for the perfect moment to strike? The Dominator seems unstoppable, a relic of the Old Empire's unstoppable might, unless...

Can Adira come up with a way to reduce the mighty ship to a drifting hulk? Will Gideon come up with a brilliant and brutal endgame and triumph over his enemy? Certainly not through sheer force, but with strategy and precision? Will he end Ivan Morozov's reign of terror in a blaze of destruction or will he and all his faithful followers perish?

Will his fleet ever make it back to Albion? Triumphant or bloodied or destroyed? The story gives readers the haunting fear that

Adira's whole fleet will become a ghostly reminder of the perils and the power of this unforgiving universe. Or will underdog Gideon Adira ascend to new heights? The question lingers—how long can a man of honor survive in a galaxy so consumed by corruption and decay?

In the Shadow of a Giant is a gripping tale of honor, betrayal, and cunning warfare set against the backdrop of a galaxy in decline. Fans of space operas like Dune and The Expanse will find themselves enthralled by the intricate politics, the fierce battles, and the richly detailed world in which Gideon Adira fights not just for survival, but for a legacy. With pulse-pounding action, high-stakes drama, and a richly textured world teetering on the edge of chaos, this short story is a must-read for anyone who craves adventure among the stars.

### Sssnake Jokessss, Riddlessss & Rattlessss - By And For Kids By Six-Year-Old Joseph Graff

Six-year-old Joseph Graff wrote these hilarious, silly, funny snake jokes inspired by his favorite cartoon saga at the time: based on an extremely long and complex- seemingly never ending - saga of ninjas fighting evil (snakes mainly).

Look for the BONUS excerpt in this book!

### God-Engines

A short story by twelve-year-old Joseph Graff August 11, 2021

## Joffe Nezum Official Wiki (No).

"Stream of conciousness", "modernist" (as pioneered by James Joyce's Ulysses, surrealist literature by young Joseph Graff

## Joesephianism Inc. (Un)Official Wiki

Novelette from the mind of eleven-year-old Joseph Graff
"I came up with this for fun, and to prove that I had the idea first. October 8th, 2020"

## The Ten Human Homeworlds

Novel by Joseph Graff

COMING SOON!!

## In The Shadow Of A Giant - An Illustrated Short Story: Sci-Fi Tale Of Noble Houses' Epic Starship Battles, Political Intrigue, Sabotage, Revenge & Ultimately, Survival In A Decaying Galactic Empire

ILLUSTRATED SHORTY STORY by Joseph Graff
Look for the NOVELETTE - same title & author!

In the Shadow of a Giant invites readers on a pulse-pounding space epic, set in a universe where remnants of a collapsed empire battle for survival and supremacy in a lawless galaxy. In the vast, empty reaches of space, a fleet of merchant starships sails under the command of Commodore Gideon Adira, a man of noble lineage but dwindling resources. His convoy, carrying precious cargo to feed the crumbling Space City Albion, must navigate treacherous star lanes, where danger lurks behind every asteroid and enemies are never far from striking.

The giant looming in this tale is literal and metaphorical—a massive, decaying space city, once the heart of an empire, now a shadow of its former glory. Its inhabitants, billions strong, teeter on the brink of starvation, relying on the courage of men like Adira to bring them supplies and fend off the marauding pirate fleets that haunt the stars. But corruption and incompetence have crippled Albion, a place where noble houses, once bastions of power, have degenerated into feudal lords bickering over scraps of power.

Enter Commodore Gideon Adira, a man born to a noble house, yet scorned by the powerful due to his family's diminished status. Unlike other commanders who rule through fear, Gideon is a man of honor in a dishonorable world, and his crew follow him with a rare loyalty. They embark on a high-stakes journey, not just for survival, but to seize an opportunity that could elevate their fortunes—an asteroid cluster rich in resources, coveted by rival houses.

But as they venture beyond the relative safety of Albion's defenses, will they find themselves in the crosshairs of Ivan Morozov, a brutal enemy from a rival house? The Dominator, a fearsome warship under Morozov's command, sets its sights on Gideon's fleet. The tension rises as a high-stakes game of cat-and-mouse unfolds, and the stakes become life and death. Morozov's savagery knows no bounds—will he capture Adira or his loyal followers? Will the Adira line end?

Gideon Adira is not a man who backs down from a fight. Won't he - using his wits and the loyalty of his well-trained crew - concoct a daring plan to finally defeat the Dominator? Or will the mighty warship bear down on the Adira convoy, pummeling it with destructive energy lances? Will Gideon hold his nerve? Will he wait for the perfect moment to strike? The Dominator seems unstoppable, a relic of the Old Empire's unstoppable might, unless...

Can Adira come up with a way to reduce the mighty ship to a drifting hulk? Will Gideon come up with a brilliant and brutal endgame and triumph over his enemy? Certainly not through sheer force, but with strategy and precision? Will he end Ivan Morozov's reign of terror in a blaze of destruction or will he and all his faithful followers perish?

Will his fleet ever make it back to Albion? Triumphant or bloodied or destroyed? The story gives readers the haunting fear that Adira's whole fleet will become a ghostly reminder of the perils and the power of this unforgiving universe. Or will underdog Gideon Adira ascend to new heights? The question lingers—how long can a man of honor survive in a galaxy so consumed by corruption and decay?

In the Shadow of a Giant is a gripping tale of honor, betrayal, and cunning warfare set against the backdrop of a galaxy in decline. Fans of space operas like Dune and The Expanse will find themselves enthralled by the intricate politics, the fierce battles, and the richly detailed world in which Gideon Adira fights not just for survival, but for a legacy. With pulse-pounding action, high-stakes drama, and a richly textured world teetering on the edge of chaos, this short story is a must-read for anyone who craves adventure among the stars.

Made in the USA
Columbia, SC
25 January 2025

77f9b540-25ad-4f25-b40a-62251c44e5ebR01